ISBN 978-1-331-32719-6
PIBN 10174787

1 MONTH OF
FREE
READING

at

www.ForgottenBooks.com

By purchasing this book you are eligible for one month membership to ForgottenBooks.com, giving you unlimited access to our entire collection of over 700,000 titles via our web site and mobile apps.

To claim your free month visit:

www.forgottenbooks.com/free174787

ALL ABOARD

FOR SUNRISE LANDS.

A TRIP THROUGH CALIFORNIA ACROSS THE PACIFIC TO JAPAN, CHINA AND AUSTRALIA.

BY

EDWARD A. RAND.

AUTHOR OF "PUSHING AHEAD;" "ROY'S DORY;" "BARK-CABIN;" "TENT IN THE NOTCH," ETC., ETC., ETC.

ILLUSTRATED.

FIFTEENTH THOUSAND.

CHICAGO:

WILLIAM M. FARRAR.

New York: FAIRBANKS, PALMER & CO. St. Louis: R. S. PEALE & Co.

1883.

CONTENTS.

LIST OF ILLUSTRATIONS.

GRAND CANON OF THE COLORADO. (6.200 *feet deep.*)

10

PREFACE.

ALL ABOARD! Wherever one may have a chance to take the cars for the West, we invite them to meet us in San Francisco and join in this proposed trip. It will cost but little; nothing for meals, or lodgings, or extra clothing, for steamboat or railroad fare. The only thing needed is the possession of the book itself, and a leisure hour under a garret-roof that the rain is tapping, or by a blazing fire in winter, or out in a swinging hammock when summer comes.

Are there not boys who like adventure, a fire and a chowder on the beach, a climb, too, up a sand-hummock, though vicious gusts and pelting rain may follow? Then all aboard for Sunrise Lands! Are there not some who are shut up in sick rooms? We feel for you, and this trip is for you also. We have spoken to the "clerk of the weather," who has promised sunny skies. There will be, though, one storm, but not a raindrop shall reach you. And the girls — do we leave them out? They are all welcome. Plenty of room for everybody. The *Antelope* is to be built in part of a new material — iron and rubber. She will last, and yet she will swell to the size of any desired passenger-load. *All*-aboard!

We would here express our indebtedness to the Rev. D. Crosby Greene, D. D. of the Japan Mission of the American Board, and one of the translators of the Japanese New Testament, for timely suggestions as to Japanese customs, and also acknowledge the courtesy of Messrs. E. W. and L. E. Page of New York city, whose experience in Australia and elsewhere in the Pacific has been a valuable one. And we want to be able to thank every one, the young and the old, for going with us. We want all to know Uncle Nat, Ralph and Rick, Jack Bobstay — but the last bell is sounding! All aboard!

E. A. R.

ALL ABOARD FOR SUNRISE LANDS.

CHAPTER I.

WHO THEY WERE.

"ALL ABOARD for Sunrise Lands! All aboard!" And wasn't it the merriest voice in the world saying this? Then it must have been Uncle Nat who gave the above invitation, for he had that kind of voice. He was calling out to his enterprising nephews, Ralph Rogers and his brother, Rick, as they took the cars at a California station for San Francisco. Ralph and Rick were Massachusetts boys whose home was in Concord. Their father had long been dead, but their mother still kept up the old home. "It's good blood, what is in you, boys," the mother would say. "You know the Concord woman in Revolutionary times, when Major Pitcairn and his British troops came to town. The court house had been set on fire, and it threatened to burn her house. She interceded with the major, her water pails in her hands, and got him to put the fire out. She belonged to our family. Blood tells, boys. Don't forget."

"No, mother, but blood won't put out fires. There has got to

13

be a *man* behind it, and mind makes the man here in America," said Ralph, one day, threatening to swell to the size of a Fourth of July speech.

"But it is in 'em, the blood after all," the mother said to herself. "Their ancestors fought at Concord Bridge."

Ralph was about fourteen, and Rick three years and a half younger. Rick was just the sort of boy to get into a scrape, enthusiastic and impulsive, and Ralph who was a bit cooler, would sometimes prove to be the very boy to get Rick out of a scrape. Rick had a face for-

CONCORD BRIDGE.

ever on the smile, his blue eyes laughing, and his mouth also, except — look out for such moments! When Rick looked sober, and talking excitedly, said, "See — see, R — Ralph! Look-er here! Couldn't you and I" — his mother did not need to hear the rest.

"Oh, dear, what is Rick up to now?" she would exclaim.

Rick's soberness meant that the mischievous thought laughing out of his eyes and mouth, had shaped itself into a plan, and would

SHE INTERCEDED WITH THE MAJOR.

soon be heard from. Ralph's face was more quiet and subdued, and his eyes were of a softer hazel, but there was the same kind of family-smile — their father had it before them — making its sunny home in the corners of both his eyes and mouth. They were generous, big-hearted boys, though inheriting from our common father, Adam, a good share of human infirmities, liking fun and their own way more than was always convenient for their mother.

"Oh, dear," she would sometimes say, "I don't know what Rick is coming to, and there is Ralph who is more steady, but he surprises me also, now and then. But there, I mean to do the best I can, and ask God to do the rest." In all this she was very sensible.

An unwelcome guest, the scarlet fever, came into the house one day, and when it had gone out again, it spitefully left Ralph and Rick very "weak and mizable" as old Nurse Fennel said. Rick's round face, whose eyes and mouth were the hiding places of constant and roguish smiles, looked quite narrow and sad, while Ralph stepped feebly as if his next request would be for a crutch.

NURSE FENNEL AT HOME.

"Yes, mizable, jest mizable them boys are, and you jest need, Miss Rogers, to give them a change of hair. A change of hair is what will fix 'em," triumphantly said Nurse Fennel. She had thought this out one day while busily knitting, at the same time offering to her tame squirrel a home in her pocket. She had lived in England in her earlier days, afterward coming to Yankee-land. Consequently, the peculiarities of dialect of the old and the new country had fastened themselves upon her like the barnacles encrusting the piers of an old wharf. "A change of what?" asked Mrs. Rogers, fancying that the old lady wanted the boys' locks to be removed. "Oh, I see now! But they take the air and walk out every day."

"I mean a journey, marm."

"A journey?" thought Mrs. Rogers. "Where can it be?"

There happened along, that very week, Uncle Nat Stevens. God bless the Uncle Nats with which he has sprinkled the world like plums in a pudding. This Uncle Nat was a man past forty, and a sea-captain. He had a stout body and a big head, a rosy face, brown eyes and a brown moustache to match them. He had much energy of manner, and he was a thorough seaman. He had helped himself and gone up rapidly from post to post; but he was ready to help others, and an old sailor said, "the cap'n was a regular chicken at heart if any one might be swamped in a rough sea and need help," for his heart matched in size his head.

The day after his arrival in Concord, the captain and Mrs. Rogers were talking about family-matters. "The boys are pretty well, but they do need a change," affirmed Mrs. Rogers.

"Ellen Maria," the captain replied in his brisk, rapid way, "you say your lambs need a change, and I don't wonder, for they look thin as a potato-skin. Now see! You know I am said to be one of those folks always along just in time to put their foot into everything."

So he was, but it was a most excellent foot he brought with him.

"Now, let me tell you what kind of a cruise I shall be up to this year. I am going to San Francisco, and there taking steamer, shall run over to Japan. At a Japanese port, I expect to find my old ship, the Antelope. She has been in other hands the past year, but when she reaches Japan, the owners wish to make a change, and

THE SUSPENSION ACT.

want me to take her again. Then I slip down through the Pacific to New Zealand, across the water to Australia, then up to Hong Kong, and afterwards I may go to India and Egypt, through the Mediterranean, home. Look here, Ellen Maria!" Ellen Maria looked.

· Now I am going to make a proposition, and that is, to let me take your two boys with me."

Ellen Maria's eyes went up and her hands went down. "Massy!" she ejaculated.

"I am in earnest, sister. You must see that your boys need something, for they are all pe-tered out. They have lost their vitality, or whatever you call it. What a dif-ference between to-day and the last time I visited you! They are quiet as lambs now, and so I called them that. There, the last time I was here, I remember one of them got caught in an apple tree back of your sitting-room window. It was hardly a case of inani-mate suspension, but the

THE BARREL ACT.

very reverse of it.   The time before, when I was at home, one of them
tumbled into a barrel, and two of his young friends came to the
rescue and fished him out.   To-day, their vitality seems all gone.
Now you let me have those boys and I will take the best care of them
while away, and bring them back to you safe and sound.   Won't they
pick up while gone, and won't they learn a lot also!"

GRANDPA ROGERS' HOME IN SUMMER.

"That is splendid in you, Nat, but how can I spare them?   Don't
whisper a word to them."

Those enterprising boys, "quiet as lambs," got hold of the plan in less
than an hour, and five minutes after knowing it, presented themselves to
their mother in their best suits, carrying an old leather trunk between

them, and in each unoccupied hand a travelling-bag, saying they wanted to bid mother good-bye before starting to find the sunrise!

That settled the matter, and in a few days, it was decided that they might accompany Uncle Nat on his trip.

"We must go to grandpa's first," said Rick.

Dear old grandpa! Like a stream coming down from a mountain-top and watering many fields, is the influence of loving grandparents over the generations below them. Grandpa Rogers lived in a house approached by one of the prettiest, and most leafy walks of summer. The trees were bare now, but the home itself was like an old oak covered with the foliage of many tender and beautiful associations.

When grandpa had been visited, Uncle Nat and his nephews left New England.

The trip to California was made, and a visit also to some California friends, the Peters. The Peters were sorry to have their Eastern visitors leave, and the boys' departure was especially regretted by a colored youth on the premises, Josiah, or Siah, as he was generally called. Siah was a stout, black boy caught up by the wave of some colored exodus from the South, and carried West by it. He had no father or mother, but had left an old aunty behind who sent after him the prayers she could not personally follow. She sent also her most dearly prized earthly treasure, a little pocket Bible. Asking her minister to pick out passages appropriate to a young person, she then drew with her own hand a big pencil-mark about them. They were admonitions after this style: "My son, if sinners entice thee, consent thou not."

As Siah could not read, he did not know just what precious stones might be in these caskets, but their nature in general, he understood, that it was "something bery good fur young folks," and it had its influence. Certain stains, too, he knew were aunty's tear-marks, and this touched him.   Aunty's Bible and a certain amount of self-respect had kept Siah, amid all his migrations, from that carelessness and coarseness so incident to such a life.   He was at work now on the farm of Mr. Peters, Uncle Nat's host, and he and the Rogers boys were excellent friends.

"I wish I could go wid ye," said Siah.   "'Pears to me as if I must."

There was no way opening itself to him, and to Siah's great regret, he was not able to join in this "hunt fur de sunrise," as he called it.   He followed them though as far as the door of the train that was to bear them away, and when the engine began to sneeze and grunt, he joined in the start, and grinning, raced as far as he could, beside the track.   Ralph and Rick turned to look at him once more, and they caught a glimpse of his face, the smile gone, his big, mournful eyes watching the vanishing train.

"There, boys, we are off at last," said Uncle Nat, "and we shall be in Oakland in three hours.   San Francisco is not far from the sea on a bay, and about half a dozen miles across the bay from San Francisco, is Oakland.   We get out at the latter place and are ferried across the bay to San Francisco."

It was evening when they took the ferry-boat for San Francisco. All about them stretched the waters of the bay, one mass of blackness, but before them flashed the lights of San Francisco, multiplying as they neared the city, brightening and sharpening, till they seemed like the many camp-fires of an army resting on the slope of a hill.

CHAPTER II.

WESTERN FREAKS.

ECHO ROCK.

SOME one was making a sound like a locomotive whistle.

"Oh – h – h – h! Isn't that steep? That's like them."

It was Rick. Hs was looking at a book of pictures lying on a table in the parlor of the San Francisco hotel where Uncle Nat was stopping. When he said, "That's like them," he meant pictures of cañons, a feature of scenery the boys saw in California.

"Do you want me to tell you about the pictures? I have been all through that country."

This interrupting voice was a very pleasant one, and it sounded directly above Rick's head. He looked up and saw a man's face over him.

"Oh — is — this your book?" asked Rick.

"Oh that is all right. Now if you would like to hear about those pictures you get that boy over there in the corner, for I guess he is your brother, and I will tell you both about them."

The stranger meant Ralph.

"Ralph," said Rick, approaching his brother, "a man is going to tell you and me about some pictures. It is a country that uncle said he was sorry to skip on his way here."

"That man?" he asked. "I know him; that man's name is Greene, for I saw him write it in the register in the office," he whispered.

LOWER CANON OF THE KANAB. (3000 *feet deep*.)

The stranger was very social.

"I want to tell you about the wonderful cañons we have in the far West. Did you ever see a cañon?"

"We saw one on our way, sir, and Uncle Nat promised some time to tell us the reason for it," remarked Ralph. "It was here in California among the mountains, and Uncle Nat has seen big, big ones in the Yosemite Valley."

"Yes, and this will illustrate the whole subject. And Uncle Nat, who is Uncle Nat?"

THE GRAND CAÑON, LOOKING WEST FROM TORO WEAP.

" He is here, and at your service, sir," said some one in the rear of the group.

The stranger turned and levelled a pair of big eye-glasses at the late arrival.

" Nat Stevens ! "

" Bill Greene ! "

" Where did you come from ? "

" And where did *you* come from ? "

" Boys, this is Mr. Greene, with whom I used to go to school years ago."

" Didn't I say it was Greene?" whispered Ralph in a tone of triumph.

When the two old school-mates had expressed their mutual pleasure at the meeting, and explained to one another their courses of travel, Mr.

GUNNISON'S BUTTE AT THE FOOT OF GRAY CAÑON. (2700 *feet high.*)

Greene resumed his talk which had been so pleasantly interrupted.

" I was going to tell the boys what caused the cañons. some of which

CLIMBING THE GRAND CAÑON. .

you have seen. Either one of you know, boys?"

"A drop of water," promptly replied Ralph.

"Pooh!" exclaimed Rick.

"But, Rick, your brother is nearer right than you would think for. These rocky valleys down through which rattle the mountain streams, may have been affected by convulsions of the earth's surface, but drops of water have certainly been at work, cutting and wearing away.

"A stream sweeps from the mountains down into the plains, and as it rolls on, it cuts like a wheel into the earth. By-and-by, the groove becomes very deep. The river Colorado has hollowed out a cañon over a thousand miles of its way.

"Here is what we term Terrace Cañons, and you can see the deep groove back through these steps or terraces. At the foot of the first terrace or step, we see the water on whose surface drift the boats of travellers of some kind. In the Grand Cañon,

BIRD'S-EYE VIEW OF TERRACE CANONS.

see what magnificent amphithea-
tres have been hollowed out in the
rock. The traveller finds traces of
volcanic action, the lava pouring
into the river-bed, and the water
cutting through the lava. It is
no trifling thing to go through
the Grand Cañon, where a fellow
is boxed between these high walls
of the river, and on he must go,
over bad places in the way, where
the water sweeps down and rushes
and whirls. Then you may come
to smooth water, one surface of
glass stretching from shore to
shore save as some long, wind-
ing ripple breaks it. It looks
pretty calm in the Gate of Lodore, does it not?"

"Oh–h! oh–h!" broke out
Ralph.

His eyes were fixed on a deep
mountain-cut, and he began to
read: "Winnie's Grotto, a side
cañon, walls two thousand feet
high." Not only were the walls
high, but there were profiles cut
out in the outlines of the rocky
walls, faces that scowled at one
another over the deep, gloomy pit,

WINNIE'S GROTTO. (2000 FEET.)

and the boys amused themselves by tracing their hard, stern lineaments.

"One beautiful cañon is Marble Cañon," said Mr. Greene. "At least two thousand five hundred feet high, are the lofty walls of marble.

INTERPRETER AND HIS FAMILY.

The shades of marble are varied, and where the water has rubbed and smoothed them, they are charming. Marble Cañon is sixty-five and a half miles long, and starting with a height of two hundred feet, this is increased to three thousand five hundred feet."

MARBLE CANON.

GATE OF LODORE.

"See that woman in black!" called out Ralph.

"That is a place," remarked Mr. Greene, "which is called Islano Monument, and it is one of the curiously-shaped rocks you will find.

They may take the form of domes, pinnacles, alcoves, sculptured cathedral walls."

RUNNING A RAPID.

" It would take a pretty good climber to go up some of those walls." remarked Uncle Nat.

"Yes if he will try, he had better borrow a pair of wings to scale certain places."

Mr. Greene went on to say, "One statement I made, I want to fill out. I spoke of the action of water in the forming of cañons and referred to other agencies. There have plainly been the latter. One day, I noticed in the Colorado, masses of lava-rock, some of them low, and yet others rose up to a height of a hundred feet and more. After a while, I came to an old dead volcano on the right of a fall in the river. From the mouth of this volcano, immense lava-streams had been discharged into the river, and it looked as if in all, a mass twelve or fifteen hundred feet deep had been poured out. Then the water cut its way through, and you can see in some places a line of basalt on either side. Here is a question that might be asked. In the forming of cañons, why did not the rivers run *round* the mountains rather than *through* them ? Water when it meets an

ISLAND MONUMENT, GLEN CANON.

obstacle is apt to avoid it, but here the river flows through the mountain. One might say the water found a split in the mountains and poured through the split, but examination shows the water has been cutting its channel. There is one theory which will stand till the next one comes along, for science, as the farmer said of his steer, is 'an uneasy crittur.' We will suppose the river to be running across the country, its surface not especially broken, when one of those changes may have taken place of which we have evidence, a wrinkling of the surface through 'the contracting or shriveling of the earth.' The wrinkle may be a long one but not high enough to turn the river from its course, which chafes against this little elevation and rubs its way through it. What now if that process goes on, the 'wrinkle' rising, but no faster than the water can cut its way? At last, you have a mountain-range going across the country, and a river flowing in a deep mountain-cut or cañon. Prof. Powell says:

MARBLE CANON.

"'The mountains were not thrust up as peaks, but a great block was slowly lifted, and from this the mountains were carved by the clouds — patient artists, who take what time may be necessary for their work. We speak of mountains forming clouds about their tops;

the clouds have formed the mountains. Lift a district of granite, or marble, into their region, and they gather about it, and hurl their storms against it, beating the rocks into sand, and then they carry them out into the sea, carving out cañons, gulches, and valleys, and leaving plateaus and mountains embossed on the surface.'

"The action of the elements in this western country is marked. A butte is a peak or elevation too high to be a hill but too low for a mountain. We have some fine ones among or near the Colo-

BUTTES OF THE CROSS IN THE TOOM-PIN WU-NEAR TUR-WEAP.

rado cañons. It is thought that the meeting of two lateral or side-cañons will account for this, and the water has thus cut out these buttes with their terraces and towers. Prof. Powell speaks of those near Labyrinth Cañon, each one 'so regular and beautiful that you can hardly cast aside the belief that they are works of Titanic art.

"'It seems as if a thousand battles had been fought on the plains

below, and on every field the giant heroes had built a monument, com-
pared with which the pillar on Bunker Hill is but a mile stone.   But no
human hand has placed a block in all those wonderful structures.   The
rain drops of unreckoned ages have cut them all from the solid rock.'"

"You saw a pretty old river, Mr. Greene," said Ralph.

"Yes, that I did."

"Did you see any Indians?" inquired Ralph.

INDIAN VILLAGE.

"Yes, we found it quite handy to have those who could interpret
for us.

"Sometimes, journeying along, we found arrow-heads, or flint chips, or
Indian trails, and then we might come to an Indian garden.   When

we had them in our company at our camp-fire one night, they told us a famous story though a pretty long one."

"What was it about?" asked Rick, eagerly.

CAMP-FIRE AT ELFIN WATER POCKET.

"The name was So-kus Wai-un-ats, told by To-mor-ro-un-ti-kai, and the first word in it was Tum-pwi-naí-ro-gwi-nump."

"Oh dear me!" thought Rick. "Guess that will do."

The others were laughing.

"Oh I know Bill Greene of old!" said Uncle Nat. "He is joking."

But he was not joking.

CHAPTER III.

STANDING ROCKS ON THE BRINK OF MU-AV CANON.

ALL his friends knew that Uncle Nat was an intelligent traveller — who read as he travelled.

The next day after the arrival in San Francisco, he said to Ralph and Rick, "I have bought you some books, and I want you to read them. They will tell you about many of the places we shall visit on your journey."

"Do you remember, uncle, about the people coming here for gold?" asked Ralph.

"Yes, that began in 1848. Gold for a long time was known to be here, but what started the great excitement was the finding of a piece of gold when they were digging for a mill-race at Coloma. That was in January, 1848, and people began to gather here that year. It was in 1849, in the spring, that a big wave of emigration swept over our land towards California. Some went over the plains, and others by the Isthmus of Panama, and others still by the long route around Cape

Horn. What the Cape Horn route may be, some poor fellows have found out to their sorrow. The vessel starting out in hope may end a wreck. The journey over the Isthmus of Panama in those days,

was no agreeable thing, amid summer-heat, and the way over the plains was very tedious. However, many went to the Land of Gold.

HOW THE VOYAGE BEGINS.

"I was a boy then, and I remember how high the gold fever ran in my New England town. A lot went off in an old whaler called the Ann Parry. I remember go-ing down to the wharf to see the party off. All the place swarmed with spectators, and those on board the whaler seemed thick as bees. They had a long voyage before them, away round Cape Horn, the old way, but who cared for that? I remember one young fellow who had

CAPE HORN.

been a tailor, but he concluded to change the first let-ter of his occupa-tion, and become sailor. He started to go up the shrouds, and for a while this tyro did very well. But he showed that he was a bungler, for his foot slipped. Fortunately he did not tumble. The people saw it, and laughed at the man who if a Jack Tar, was plainly just out of the tar-pot. Well, a great many came here to California from every quarter, and California became a famous place. A big, fine city has grown up here."

Frequent excursions were made by Uncle Nat and his nephews from their hotel. They visited the Presidio, Seal Rock, Woodward's Garden, Lone Mountain Cemetery, Golden Gate Park, and climbed the sand hills that wall off the city from the Pacific.

"O uncle, take us to the Chinese quarter!" besought Ralph.

"Chinese quarter, Ralph? All right, I will," and Uncle Nat took them the very day he was asked. They saw the little 'shops where the butcher sells his pork cut in such queer pieces, displaying also his chicken and fish, where the tea dealer peddles his choice herb, and the clothier his funny tunics or blouses.

"And — what is that?" asked Rick. "My!"

"That's a joss-house," said Uncle Nat.

"Joss-house? What do they call it that for?"

"The Portuguese for God is deos, and the imperfect pronunciation of this by the Chinese gives the word joss."

They looked inside. It was some festival-day, for many people were there. On the walls of the house were queer decorations, and near the door, was a big bell that a Chinaman struck. There were ugly images to represent the good and the evil powers, also the man cast out of heaven, and before these, sandal-wood tapers were burning.

"The Chinese," explained Uncle Nat, "believe in two powers, good and bad. The good, they reason, will be friendly any way. It is the bad that will harm them, and must receive special attention and be propitiated. Consequently they try to keep the latter quiet and well-disposed. Knowing how powerful is the influence of a good dinner,

they offer food of various kinds, and this explains the dishes you will see in a joss-house. Then they have a certain course of life which they feel they must lead, that they may secure peace hereafter, provided the evil one does not interfere. But that they may not be expelled from the Chinese heaven hereafter, they keep in the joss-house the image of the man that was cast out of heaven, as a reminder."

THE MINUTE MAN.

After the visit to the joss-house, Uncle Nat stepped into a store to make a purchase, leaving Rick and Ralph on the sidewalk. With their customary impulsiveness, they decided it could do no harm to go ahead a little way; and having inspected the neighborhood they could then return to Uncle Nat.

"What's that?" asked Ralph, as they turned a corner. In the street was a young Chinaman in a blue tunic and baggy blue trousers. He was carrying a basket that must have contained a heavy article, for he often shifted the basket from hand to hand as if it hurt

him. He passed a group of street urchins, who evidently began at once
to plot mischief.   Soon a boy ran up to him, and giving his tunic or
blouse an energetic pull, rushed to the other side of the street.   When the
young man turned to face his aggressor, a second boy from an opposite
quarter rushed up unnoticed and gave a second fierce pull.   Like a vane
shifting about on a very squally day, and obeying the new current that impels it, the Chinaman turned to notice this new invasion. But then a third assailant came up on the side of the first attack, pulling and jostling — a fourth arrived and a fifth even — the young man struggling in their midst like a hen with a parcel of hawks. He did not dare put down his basket even for a moment, aware that the harpies would have immediately clutched it, and his retention of his property made resistance all the more difficult. Ralph and Rick were

THE GOOD WOMAN.

' boys living in a town that had a statue of the " Minute man " of revolutionary days ready at a moment's notice to fly to arms and resist Britain's
overshadowing power, and they were not going to see the weaker side
in a fight — be it Chinaman or freedman — crowded under foot.

   " Come on, Rick! " shouted Ralph.

   Rick generally went off at a bound any way, but if he saw Ralph
ahead,. he would spring all the quicker.   And away he went after

HOW THE VOYAGE MAY END.

Ralph, rushing and shouting. Ralph grabbed a boy who had seized the basket, and repeating an old trick which he had practised on almost every one at home till they were about crazy, he neatly inserted his foot between the boy's legs and tripped him up. There was now a fresh uproar. Round a street corner came a reinforcement of three street Arabs longing for an opportunity to stretch their idle muscles.

Matters threatened to become very serious for Ralph and Rick. Suddenly, Uncle Nat appeared. His big, brawny form rose above the assailants threateningly, as a broom over a cloud of mosquitoes.

" Away with ye," he shouted, seizing a couple of boys by the collar at once.

Was it a giant-torpedo exploding in their midst ? It certainly had the effect of one. The hornet swarm broke up immediately, leaving the young Chinaman alone with his defenders.

JOE.

" Look here, boys ! " said Uncle Nat to his enterprising nephews. " Don't stray off so. Just wait for me and then when we see any of the enemy about, we will charge on them all together and rout them gloriously. There goes Joe Pigtail ! "

" Is that his name ? " asked Rick, looking wonderingly at the boy.

" No, Rick, but that will identify him to us. What grateful bows he gave us ! Let's follow him."

When the newly named Jòe Pigtail saw that they were following him, he stopped and waited for them.

"We wanted to look about Chinatown," said Uncle Nat to Joe.

"Chinee-town? Goodee. Me showee," and he kindly led them to quarters they had not seen and to other queer shops, finally stopping before a house that had a laundry look.

"Me — me!" he said, intimating that he stopped there, and beckoning them in.

In the outer room there were three men busy with laundry-work, and through an open door a fourth could be seen occupied with some kind of cooking in his shadowy cubby-hole. In the outer room, everything was very plain, and though there was an abundance of chances to stand up, there was none to sit down unless one literally took the floor. A side door into a yard had been swung back and looking across this yard the boys could see into the next house where a middle-aged American lady was seated beside a Chinese boy teaching him out of a book.

"She goodee woman — like you!" said Joe to Uncle Nat in complimentary tones.

"Uncle Nat ain't a woman," whispered Rick to Ralph.

When they left the place, turning to look back, they saw Joe standing by a laundry table and gazing thoughtfully upon the retreating party.

CHAPTER IV.

AT SEA.

SUNSET AT GOLDEN GATE AND FORT POINT.

THE City of Tokio, a vessel belonging to the Pacific Mail Steamship Co., was lying at her wharf. Men were hurrying about, giving or obeying orders. The last trunks were going on board. People were saying good-bye, while the fizz of escaping steam that could be heard, plainly said, that the leviathan was impatient to be off. Everything was ready at last. Every fastening was released and one Saturday in early spring the steamship gracefully, majestically moved away.

"Hurrah!" shouted Rick enthusiastically, as he stood among the passengers watching every movement.

"Hurrah!" shouted Ralph.

"Hurrah!" responded Uncle Nat and the other passengers, while a group of enthusiastic boys on shore joined in three ringing cheers.

In a few moments the pilgrims for the Sunrise were moving rapidly down the bay.

"There are some sailing craft ahead, boys. They look slow, don't they, boys, old-fashioned and behind the times, beside this craft. This is the nineteenth century," observed Uncle Nat.

Just then the City of Tokio blew her whistle and she seemed to shriek, "Yes, I'm the nineteenth century and I'll beat and cross the Pacific, see if I don't." She said this in one long breath, gasped and said no more.

"There is the Golden Gate!" exclaimed Uncle Nat. "What a pretty sight!"

Between two ridges of land stretched the waters of the Golden Gate, and outside was the broad and shining sea.

"This is the entrance to the bay of San Francisco, boys; and there is the Pacific we must cross. Can't you say the lines you repeated at the hotel the other night?"

Ralph was proud of his accurate memory, and he recited the lines he had recently seen among Bret Harte's poems:

> "Serene, indifferent of Fate
> Thou sittest at the Western Gate.
>
> Upon thy heights so lately won,
> Still slant the banners of the sun,
>
> Thou seest the white seas strike their tents,
> O warder of two continents?
>
> And scornful of the peace that flies
> Thy angry winds and sullen skies,
>
> Thou drawest all things small or great,
> To thee, beside the Western Gate."

The boys were so much interested in their new surroundings that

THE CITY OF TOKIO.

they were sorry to see the sun sinking toward the western rim of the sea.

"I would like," said Ralph, "to have that sun catch on some peg in the clouds, and hold on awhile. Oh, Uncle Nat, didn't you once say you saw the sun keep up above the sea and not go down at night?"

"Yes, and it was so strange to have the watch say eight, nine, ten, eleven, twelve o'clock at night, and still see the sun shining,

IN HIGH NORTHERN LATITUDE.

shining in the west. It was worth the journey I took in a high northern lat-

itude to accomplish the feat.   In any Arctic country, it must be strange
to a person from the Southern land to see the sun day after day wheel
round the heavens.   In Greenland, the sun is always above the horizon
in June and July, and then there are days where his absence is only
long enough to give him a little dip below the horizon and up he comes
again.   While it is summer in Greenland, and that season exceeds four
months only in few places, vegetation makes great advances."

When night came, they were out upon the bosom of the Pacific.
The big steamer steadily made its way over the lonely, darkening waters.
The stars brought forward their tapers one by one and lighted up the
windows of the sky.   The wind came in chilly breaths.   The dull,
heavy swash of the waters about the vessel could be heard.   Our three
pilgrims were fairly afloat, going west as Uncle Nat said, to find the
east; moving toward the sunset to search out the sunrise lands.

The boys saw the moon rise above the water.

"Uncle Nat," asked Rick, "why are there so many moons, a family
of moons with different faces, and not one thing looking the same all
the time?"

"Come into my state-room."

In the state-room, Uncle Nat took a book out of his trunk and
showed the boys a picture of the sun, the earth, and also the moon at
different points in its journey about the earth.

"There in that outside circle is the moon as it appears to the sun,
now showing a bright surface.   But in the inner circle is the moon
at different points as it appears to the earth.   Take when the moon is
between the earth and the sun, and we have the moon's dark side
turned toward us, or we get no moon at all.   But a little farther
along, we catch a bit of the moon's bright side like a crescent, and farther along — "

"Oh, I see!" shouted Rick.   "It is easy enough now, after you know. And when the moon is round on the side opposite where you started, we get the whole of the bright side, or it is full moon. Goodie, goodie!"

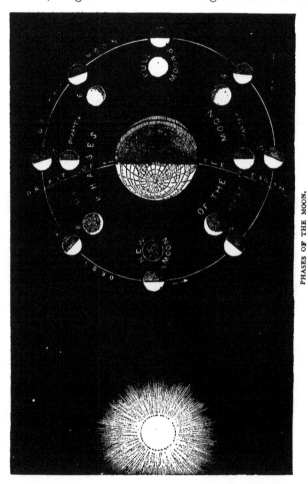

PHASES OF THE MOON.

"You have got it now, Rick," said Uncle Nat, smiling at his nephew's enthusiasm.

"Ralph, do you understand?"

Ralph nodded his head but looked glum; "I — I — don't feel right — here," and he laid his hand on his stomach.

"Ah, *it* is coming on, I see. Well, I will put you right to bed, and fix you all nice."

The mysterious "it" soon made Rick put his hand to his stomach, and Uncle Nat had his hands full for a time.

CHAPTER V.

DISCOVERIES.

PEOPLE on board a steamer easily become acquainted, and Ralph and Rick were disposed to know everybody. Recovering from their "touch of seasickness," as Uncle Nat termed it ("a touch heavy enough to knock a feller over," Rick thought) they were continually making exploring expeditions. They would take a peep at the engineer, then look at the furnaces, then at the cook's quarters, finally mounting to the saloon. After a while, back they would go, nodding once more at the engineer, and then fetching up near the furnaces. The third afternoon out, Ralph had circumnavigated the steamer several times, and finally stopped to watch the furnaces. Only one person seemed to be at work there, and he was shoveling up the big lumps of coal preparatory to a feeding of the red, angry furnace-mouths. The shoveling ceased, and now from a dusty corner, Ralph heard a series of noises, a rat squealing, a cat mewing as if hungry for the rat, and then a dog growling as if hungry for cat and rat both. At the same time, what did he see? A lump of coal that had flashing eyes, open mouth and white teeth? There were several appearances and disappearances of this kind, and Ralph thought that it went ahead of any "magic exhibition" that the Rogers brothers had ever given in the old barn at Concord. "It is gone!" said Ralph. "No, there it is!" Again, he saw the face, and heard a lion roaring as if in full pursuit of dog, cat and rat. Ralph had seen and heard enough in this magic-haunted spot and turned to leave it, when a familiar and pleasant voice said, "Chile, don't you know me?"

"Siah!" exclaimed Ralph. "It's Siah! It's Siah!" he shouted.

It was indeed the rollicking, laughing Siah who came out of the shadows in the corner, at the same time that he took down his coal-shovel screening his face. He came forward with a funny air of self-importance as if he were the ruler of Soudan showing himself to his subjects.

"Don't you see it is your ole frien', Siah?"

"Yes, but how did you get here?" asked Ralph.

"Well. I couldn't get here without doin' some walkin', sartin sure. So much to begin wid. You see after you left it was awful lonesome roun' de place, an' I jes' axed Massa Peters ef he couldn' spare me. An' he said, he hated to hab me fur to go, but ef I couldn' be contented, I might go. So I trabeled on—"

"Not all the way on foot?"

Yes, the ardent Siah had footed it to San Francisco.

"I felt like takin' a sea-viyage wid my frien's, I tole de boss — dat's Massa Peters — an' trab'lin' here, I foun' out de steamer dat was gwine, an' I knew from what you said which one it was, an' I jes' hired out as one ob de han's. You know I want fur to see de worl', an' ef I do I must begin early. Den it gibs me a chance to see you and your libely bruder."

And so Siah was following his friends to Japan. What he would do when arriving there, he had not considered.

"Dat question," he told Ralph, "am too many days off. I might be dead 'fore den, an' de question not hab any importance. So I won't raise de question till I get dar."

"It's Siah! Siah! It's Si—ah, Rick!" shouted Ralph.

A hurried sound of feet was heard in a moment, and two men came rushing up.

"Where, where?" they asked.

"Where is what?" said Ralph.

"Fi—re? Quick!"

"Oh it's Si—ah, I said."

"Nonsense! The next time you holler, take your dinner out of your mouth," and the men retreated in disgust.

"Ef he had some dinner in his mouth, he'd be more pleasant. Guess he's hungry," said Siah.

Rick now appeared, and together he and Ralph rejoiced over their treasure found once more.

"Uncle Nat," said Ralph, "Siah told me a lot about the fire-room and the fires there, and it was real interesting."

"Did he tell you anything so interesting as the kindling of fires when you have nothing to light them with?"

"Nothing to light them with, Uncle!" exclaimed Rick. "That is not very likely."

"The savages do it though. Capt. Cook found a drilling process common among the Australians, where they took a stick of dry, soft wood, and setting it on another piece, twirled it between their hands, the friction producing fire in less than two minutes. The Sandwich Island method is the same in principle, and also that among the Gauchos of Buenos Ayres, though the last place one end of the rubbing-stick against the breast as a carpenter would his bit. The Esquimaux, an old navigator said, pointed his stick

Drilling Process.

Swiss pump-drill.

Esquimaux Method.

Iroquois Method.

Method in use among the Gauchos of
Buenos Ayres.

Sandwich Island Method. Blunt stick
run back and forth in groove

FUNNY WAYS OF MAKING A FIRE.

with stone, and twirled by means of a strip of leather, in this way boring into stone even. In Switzerland, an apparatus has been used called the 'Pump-drill,' the hand bringing a cross-piece down that unwinds a cord and sends the spindle round. When the hand is lifted, the cord is rewound and so on. The Iroquois used a similar instrument."

When Siah was told of this, he said, "Smart folks in dis world, honey."

It was Rick's turn to make a discovery the next day. He had strayed among the Chinese passengers on board, and some of these were moving a quantity of heavy freight in that part of the steamer.

"A—hoo—hoo!" shouted a celestial to Rick who was unpleasantly near a rolling barrel. Rick did not hear. His mouth open, a smile sweeping over his face and wrinkling it, he stood watching one of the Chinese who was tickling the ear of a sleeping country-man with a chip. The barrel was quite near the unconscious Rick when a Chinaman rushed forward and seizing him drew him aside. Then Rick's friend stood grinning and bowing as if an old acquaintance.

"Why, Joe Pigtail!" said Rick. "You here?"

"Me—ee here," answered Joe. "You go—ee over to my coun—tree?"

"No, I am going to Japan."

"Me see you."

"Yes, I hope so, and I will tell my brother and Uncle Nat."

Siah and Joe Pigtail on board! How the attractions of steamship-life were multiplying! Now if they could make the acquaintance of a sailor and get him to "spin some yarns," happiness for the Rogers brothers would be complete. But where could they find "him?" They investigated the merits of several candidates. One though was pronounced "dirty." A second had a "squeaky voice," an infirmity not generally favorable to yarn-telling. "Crosser than pison," was the comment on a third. The fifth day out, Rick said mysteriously to Ralph. "I have found him; Come!" Rick led Ralph away and pointed out a grizzled old tar who was coiling up a rope, his back turned to the boys.

"Ain't he chuncky?" whispered Rick.

Suddenly, the "chuncky" sailor turned. He had a big head, or as Ralph told Rick, "He spread a good deal of sail in his face." The lower part of his face was fringed with a gray beard, and he carried at the neck a black kerchief, with immense ends. Under the heavy eyebrows of gray, there were two kindly lights that twinkled. "Blue lights," Ralph called them, "like those that a feller in trouble on the water at night would be glad to see. Something like a lighthouse."

"Hullo, boson!" the sailor sang out to Rick. "You here again?"

This title, "boson," tickled Rick.

"Yes, sir; and here's my brother Ralph."

Ralph held out his hand; "How do you do, Mr. —— " he hesitated, not knowing what to call this big lump of salt pork.

"Bobstay! Jack Bobstay, that's my name for young folks, and Jack is glad to see you."

"And what is it for old folks?" asked Rick.

"Ah, no matter about them. In this case they are not to be taken into account. What my name may be, don't make the difference of a button on a mermaid's best go-to-meeting gown. Jack Bobstay at your service!"

Here the old sailor made a low bow.

Ralph and Rick were delighted with Jack Bobstay, and they eagerly introduced him to Uncle Nat, Siah and Joe Pigtail. The Rogers brothers felt that their circle of acquaintance was widening.

CHAPTER VI.

LIGHTHOUSES.

A BELL BOAT.

"BOYS," said Uncle Nat, after supper one evening, "if you will come into my state-room at once, I will show you some pictures of lighthouses, and tell you all I know upon the subject."

The invitation was accepted eagerly, and there were two pair of bright, searching eyes turned toward the pictures that Uncle Nat pointed out.

"In the first place, where rocks or shoal water may be, we have beacons or buoys if they will answer. We make beacons of stone and then again of wood or iron. A very common kind of bouy is simply a spar anchored at one end, and that we call a spar-buoy. Buoys may be of iron, and in that case are made hollow and will float. I know of dangerous rocks off Boston Harbor called the Graves, and a horn-buoy has been put there. The sea, when uneasy and moving, forces the air into this horn, and what a solemn groan it has! Then a bell-boat may be used, and the motion of the waves will keep the bell dismally sounding. We must have something in such places, for the risks are great and a wreck is an ugly sight for the sailor.

FIRST CLASS LIGHTSHIP WITH STEAM FOG WHISTLE.

"Sometimes a lightship·is used as in this picture. Such a vessel must be strongly built, one too that will swing easily at anchor, and be in readiness to meet any emergencies arising from her perilous position. You can see the chain-cable that moors this one. and she has a steam fog-whistle with which she keeps piping away in the mist. The light she shows at night is carried at the mast-head. You notice the uneasy throw of the waters around her, showing that shoal sea is close at hand. Off in the distance is a steamer, and a sailor with a spy glass is trying to make her out. Now we come to the lighthouse, and this picture is one on Mt. Desert. It is of the ordinary kind, a tower built on a

MT. DESERT LIGHTHOUSE.

69

good strong foundation, and it is doing excellent service with its warning beams. Near by, tossing in the angry waters, is a fragment of a mast, and the moonlight shows a vessel away off, that looks as if in a ticklish position. A structure like this is common, but here is one that is simply a house on a solid base of stone-work, and in the cupola of the house is the lantern. It is a Long Island Sound light. Rather a lonesome home that would be for you, boys.

FOURTH ORDER LIGHTHOUSE, AT PENFIELD L. I. SOUND.

"A modern style of lighthouse is one resting on iron piles strength-ened by braces. This is a picture of the lighthouse at Thimble Shoal, Hampton Roads, Va. On one side, there is a ladder descending to the sea, and on the other, they hoist and lower their boats. In Boston Harbor is a light that makes you think of this, called Bug Light. At a distance, you fancy it is a beetle crawling over the water toward you. I can testify that this beetle has bright eyes on dark nights.

"The modern style — many-legged or centipede style as I call it,

LIGHTHOUSE AT "THE THIMBLE SHOAL," HAMPTON ROADS, VA.

will do unless the sweep of the water is like that at Minot's Ledge, near Boston, and then they had better substitute something else. Minot's Ledge is a few miles from the entrance of Boston Harbor, an ugly stretch of ledge out into the sea. It is a bad place in a gale. and the waves thrust up their ragged white arms as if to tear the lighthouse down. When I was a boy, a structure was put up that rested on piles of iron, and it did very well for a time but a fearful storm came up that raged terribly along the New England coast. I remember I went from school, my green satchel in my hand, down to the old wharves at home to see the great tide in that storm. I never saw such tides there, before nor since. I remember they rose up and swept clear over wharves supposed to be high enough out of water always. In that storm, the fancy piece of pipe-stem on Minot's Ledge went over, the iron piles snapping like dry pine twigs. The waves were so strong that they rolled

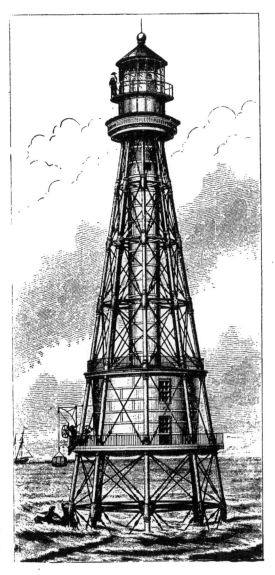

A MODERN STYLE OF LIGHTHOUSE.

ashore stone weighing one or two tons. The keepers, poor fellows, went with the wreck. When Minot's Ledge was occupied again, they gave up the pipe-stem style and built of stone, tier upon tier, solid and true. As you can only work upon the ledge at a certain stage of the tide, it took several seasons to prepare the foundation and lay a few courses of granite. But it was finished at last, and a splendid pile of granite it is."

" Uncle, what is it they light up the lantern with ? "

"Do you mean, Rick, how they do it ? Let me go back some way. There is at the mouth of the river Garonne in France, a lighthouse nigh three hundred years old, and it is a fine structure. For a light, at first they burnt pieces of oak in a chauffer or small furnace. That was a common mode, and long practised. It seemed a wonderful advance, when over this little bonfire up in the lighthouse tower, a rough reflector in the shape of an inverted cone was suspended and prevented the upward passage of the light. In 1760, Smeaton, the famous engineer of the Eddystone lighthouse, used wax candles. In 1789, in the old Garonne lighthouse, a Frenchman, Lenoir, put mirrors or reflectors near Argand lamps introduced into the lantern. The Argand lamp has a circular wick and chimney. By-and-by, in the present century, came Fresnel who made extensive improvements, introducing what is called the lens principle. A lens is any substance that will let the light through and refract or bend it. For instance, when a piece of glass is convex as we say, or when it bulges out, that will so bend the image of an object as to enlarge it. In telescopes and microscopes, we take advantage of this magnifying principle, and the big lens in the lighthouse tower is so constructed that the light of a lamp comparatively small is magnified into the shining of a mammoth ball of fire, till it seems like a new-risen sun above the dark surface of the sea. I have

gone by Minot's Light in the night, and how thankful I have been
for that big torch away out in the dangerous sea."

"What a lot Uncle Nat knows!" said Rick to Ralph when they
were by themselves. "Yes, said Ralph with a wise air, "and I will
tell you how it happened. Mother says when Uncle Nat went to sea,
he would spend his leisure time reading. That is the way boys ought
to do," he added, exercising an older brother's privilege and annexing a
suggestion intended for the benefit of the careless and ignorant youth,
Rick. "That is the way to rise in this world."

HOW UNCLE NAT SPENT HIS LEISURE HOURS.

CHAPTER VII.

JACK BOBSTAY SPINNING YARNS.

WALRUS.

HOW would you like to have me unwind a skein of yarn?" asked Jack Bobstay one day, his "blue lights" twinkling.

"A story?" replied Ralph.

Jack nodded his head.

"O just let me get Rick and see if Siah can't come too," pleaded Ralph.

There was an abundance of help in the care of the furnaces, and Siah was granted a brief furlough. Rick was always ready for any promising digression.

In a short time Ralph and Rick were curled up inside a big coil of rope, making two round lumps, like two pumpkins in a basket.

On one side of this coil, squat upon the deck, was Siah, and on the right was Jack Bobstay.

Jack began: "I have followed the sea more than these thirty years, but the toughest weather that I ever saw was on a whalin' voyage."

"You been to the North Pole?" asked Ralph.

"Pretty well up, my boy, but not jest to the peakit end of it," replied Jack.

A VESSEL TURNING INTO AN ICICLE.

77

"Did you ever see a Greenlander?" asked Rick.

"O yes, I have seen 'em shooting seals and sea lions 'round among blocks of ice."

"Did you use to go a-whalin' much?" asked Siah.

"Whalin'? I have seen more whales than you ever dreamed of, boy," said Jack with an expression almost like contempt.

"I don't know as I eber dreamed ob any," said Siah in a subdued way.

"You have forgotten your dreams, maybe;" replied Joe, disposing of dreams and dreamers with a wave of his hand.

"How far north did you ever go?" asked Rick. "Did you say you got on top of the North Pole?"

Joe disliked to own that he had not achieved anything possible or impossible. He now merely said that he must have gone "pretty near it," for he remarked with impressive dignity, "I went chuck into the jaws of the ice and snow. I have been in one or two explorin' expeditions."

"You have?" said Rick in tones of positive admiration.

"Sartin!" declared Joe with great dignity, thoroughly aware of the important place he occupied in their regard. "It is a tough position to be in; sometimes awful skittish! You see it is pretty uncomfortable to be sailin' in a vessel where masts, rigging, shrouds and sails may be covered with ice. The spray freezes as it falls, and a vessel looks at last as if she was turnin' into a big icicle. I was in one ship that went after Sir John Franklin."

"What, the man that never came back?" inquired Ralph.

"Yes, in one of them ships, for though not so thick as sandpeeps on a summer beach, still there were more than one of 'em, upward of twenty going in eleven years. You know Sir John Franklin went off in 1845, with two vessels, the Erebus and Terror, to find that humbug-place, a nor'west passage. He expected to be back in 1847, but he was never seen after July, 1845. Well, they hunted and found traces of Franklin's party on King William's Land. The Esquimaux had seen some of 'em, but what the savages had to tell, only proved that Franklin's party was at last swept away by death. I was in one of the expeditions that hunted for Sir John. You see his wife, Lady Jane, could not give him up, and when it was useless to think he could be found alive, then she spent her money trying to get some information of his fate and recover his body. When I went, I thought I might never come back myself, and then what Lady Jane would have hunted for poor Jack Bobstay? At one time, our cap'n concluded to send some of his men ahead to see what the prospect was. We had two boats, and contrived to get ahead some way, when we were caught in the sudden closing of the ice. There we were a number of miles from the ship, in two open boats, with few provisions beside our water-kegs. We drew our boats up on the ice and waited for the next thing, and that was the

A SLEEPING-BAG.

dark. Luckily, we had some sleeping bags."

"What are those?" asked Rick.

"Just what I say, bags, to sleep in. There is a chance for you to get into them — and they are made nice and warm—and when inside, you button yourself in.

"We went to sleep, and as things were no better, the next day we concluded to abandon one boat and drag the other over the ice to open water, if we could find it. We began to strip one boat, and I remember it fell to me to roll along the water-keg. Tom Savin took the sleeping-bags. Another man took the oars, and so on. Then

we fell to and helped work, along the other boat. It was no easy
job, but we managed to worry her along, now and then findin' a
leetle water that would help us, and finally we struck a channel

that led us down to the neighborhood of the ship. It was good
to set foot on her deck once more, but we were not out of all
trouble yet. We soon fell into bad company, that is, got among a
lot of icebergs and driftin' floes of ice. Them icebergs were
glorious, on both sides of you, boys, rising up like mountains and
towers, and meetin'-houses! That was one way to look at them
things and the other was, what if their cold, white jaws should
close on you and nip you up for good? We got out two boats — and
we were 'mazin' spry, I tell you — and riggin' up a tow-line, rowed
our craft out of danger. We all took a long breath when we had
'cleared that spot."

ICEBERGS ON EVERY SIDE.

Jack's breathless auditors now indulged in the same luxury.

"Did you make any acquaintances up there?" asked Rick whose social nature "abhorred a vacuum" like a desert place.

"Any acquaintances? It is not a very social place up there, and you couldn't reasonably expect to find large settled towns up in the snow and ice, and have people row out to you in the stream and ask you ashore to take dinner, and then pass the night," answered Jack with a laugh.

"But some folks must be there," persisted Rick.

"Must be some Skim-mer-hose," observed Siah learnedly.

"Esquimaux? O you see them now and then, but scatterin'-like you know. You may be sailin' along and you'll see 'em paddlin' about in their boats. They are master-hands for a boat, or kayaks as they call 'em. A kayak is intended to carry only one person, and is sixteen feet long say, not over a foot deep, sometimes but nine inches, and in the middle it may measure eighteen inches or

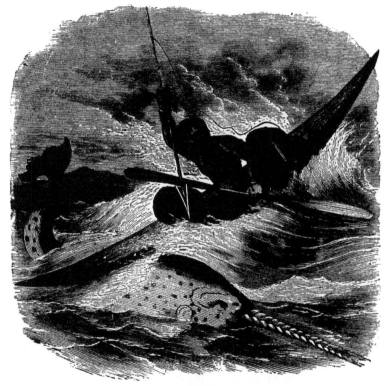

A KAYAK.

two foot across. The frame of one that I saw was made of light wood and was entirely covered with tanned sealskin."

" Cubbered all ober?" asked Siah. "Whar do der Skim-mer-hose get in?"

"In the centre is a hoop of bone that is big enough to let a man's body through, and the proprietor sits there. In the boat I inspected, he seemed to be laced in, the lower edge of his jacket being laced to the rim of the hole. Then the water is kept out. The feller had one oar about six feet long, broad like the blade of a paddle at each end, and how they managed that ticklish boat without a keel you see, I couldn't understand, but manage they did. They would go shootin' over the waters, when the spray was flyin' and the sea rough."

" But that is not the only kind of boat they have there," observed Ralph. " So I have read."

" Not the only one? Of course not," promptly replied Jack who did not mean to be found napping on the subject of Arctic navigation. " They have what they call an oomiak, and that is a woman's boat, sometimes twenty-five feet long and a third as broad. It will carry twenty people then. Sometimes they have a sail for the oomiak."

" A sail?" inquired Siah. " Where dey git de clof?"

"Inside the walrus, boy. The walrus is one of their factories for furnishin' cloth. You heard me say they covered their kayaks with seal skin, and now the walrus is another factory. I think the Esquimaux are excellent boatmen, but I don't know as I like to see one of 'em flyin' along over the water in a kayak, though interestin', any better than an Indian skimmin' over the ground on snow-shoes," observed Jack skilfully changing the subject and temptingly inviting his auditors to the consideration of another subject.

" Snow shoes!" cried Rick, his eyes steadily enlarging. " Did you ever see an Indian on snow-shoes?"

How he envied Jack!

"Plenty of 'em," remarked Jack with the air of one used to these wonders and taking them as a matter of course. "One winter I was up in Canada, away up, spendin' the season in a loggin' camp, and some Indians came pretty near us. They were out huntin' and wore snow-shoes."

"I saw a picture," said Ralph eagerly, "where an Indian was on snow-shoes, and he had just let an arrow fly at his game and had—had—"

"Pegged it;" interposed Jack. "That is what an Indian hunter is quite likely to do. Snow-shoes are simple things, the curve being

something like that of an egg. For the frame, white ash makes a good wood, and then strips of hide make a firm light nettin' on which to plant the foot. The foot is secured to the shoe at the toe, leaving the heel free to play up and down, and that lets the snow-shoe slide right along the ground."

Jack's knowledge of the snow-shoe was almost exhausted and he was endeavoring to call up another subject for the delight of his auditors, when the wondering and almost worshipping Siah spoke up; " I 'spose you've been in de water ? "

" Of course, sartin !   We sailors don't make more of that than you land folks make of stepping out on the ground," replied Jack with an almost contemptuous air.   " But," he prudently added, " we have our preferences about the quantity of water we take and *when* and *where* we get into it.   Once I was jest home from a whalin' trip, and as I had been through almost everything, I naturally felt that I was equal to any water-ventur' at home, and I took a common sail-boat intendin' to enjoy a little trip down our river, and then out to sea a

JACK WHEN SPILLED OUT.

mile or two, and so home again.   I got along very well till I reached the mouth of the river when one of the worst squalls I ever knew blew for about twenty 'minutes.   It blew all ways at once, nor-west, sow-west, nor-east, sow-east, so it seemed to me, and the sky was black as the bottom side of the cook's b'ilers.   Well, I got into a place, a bad place, where the tide and eddy meet, and over I went ! There I was spilled over about as entirely as a man

could be.   Didn't things look dark?   The waves broke lively over the rocks at the mouth of the harbor, and jest above the water was a strip of white light that made the sea and sky look all the blacker. Well, bare-headed, I paddled round till I was tired, and the squall too, and pilot-boat comin' along, they fished me up and took me home."

"Did — did you let the sail go when the squall — squall struck you — you? That's the way we do on Concord River," said Ralph eager to impart information.

"I did it every time, every time, boy, but you see I was in a bad place where tide and eddy meet. People joked me when I got back, about my knowledge of the sea, but I told 'em they were welcome to the laugh as long as I had saved my skin. Things though did not look so bad as when I was in the Nancy Dee."

"De Nancy Dee, a woman?" inquired Siah.

"A love-scrape? Massy, boy, I hope not. Jack Bobstay has not been captured yet. A ship, a ship, I mean, and a wreck, a true one, a live one."

"O tell us about that?" pleaded Ralph.

Jack's "blue-lights" twinkled, and he was evidently delighted to unwind one more yarn.

The boys now crept closer to this magnetic son of the sea who began the fascinating tale of Jack Bobstay and the Nancy Dee.

"We were nearin' the coast of England when a fearful storm struck us. It howled all day and then it blew all night. What a night that was, black and roarin', tossin' and ravin', and toward mornin', we struck! What it was then, we did not know. As it neared toward day-break, we could make out somewhat where we were. We were not far from as ugly and black a set of coast-rocks as I ever see, and we knew we were on some kind of a ledge. I've been north, south, east, west, but I never see an angrier

sea. You know when folks are mad, they sometimes grow white in
the face, and that is the way it was with that sea, white in its
anger. Nothin' but bilin' foam between us and the shore, a kind
of immense snow-drift all broken up into feathery flakes and flyin'
toward the shore! I don't know but what the light we did have
came more from that big batch of foam than from the day itself,
for the sky in the east was black as if in mournin'. We were
in a bad fix. We had been cuttin' away the mainmast and the
mizzen mast, and in fallin' they took away part of the foremast.
We looked ragged enough, and how the seas did sweep that deck!
What was to be done? No boat could live a minute in that sea,
and what headway could a swimmer make? Now when I was in
the river, that time I told you about, I felt tol'ably easy for I
could keep a-goin' till help came, but in this sea it seemed as it
the billers would chop a feller up less than no time. All at once,
something bright went over our heads! It was a rocket! Guns!
we couldn't hear it whizz, but we could see its trail and that was
jest as comfortin', and it went like a comit through the air! I
have seen fireworks, but never did I see any that did me so much
good. That rocket, you see, came from some people on the shore,

high up on the rocks, and at last we could
make out two men. Then by-and-by, there
were more. Another rocket came, and this
time it fetched a rope that fell right across
our ship. We knew what it meant. Finally
there came a life-basket. This is suspended
from a rope that goes from the ship to the
shore, and slides along this rope, so that it can
be filled at the ship and then pulled ashore.

LIFE-BASKET.

It is sometimes very difficult to reach a wreck with a life-boat, and

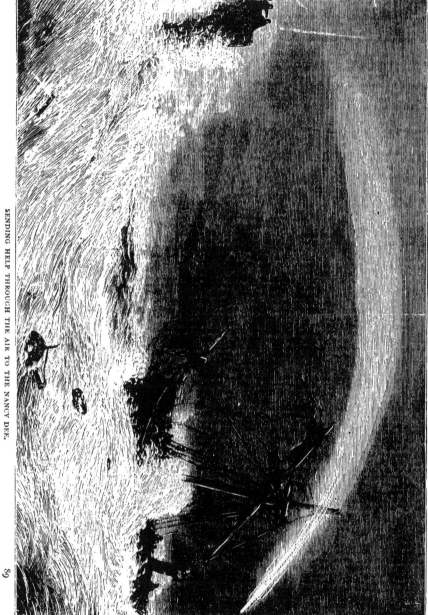

SENDING HELP THROUGH THE AIR TO THE NANCY DEE.

89

a life-basket when it can be brought into play, is much better. As for us, you may be sure that we filled our basket repeatedly, and in this way we all escaped from the Nancy Dee, that threatened to

become a good-sized coffin for us all."

The audience gave an exclamation of relief at the release of their beloved idol from danger. It would have been a congratulatory shout if he had revealed the fact that he was the last man to leave the ship and take his turn at a basket-ride. His modesty might have been overcome, had he not suddenly looked off upon the ocean and then tossing up his head, ejaculated, "Whew! There she blows!"

Saying this, he sprang to his feet. What could be the matter? "A whale, boys, a whale!" Off in the distance, they saw a white mass rising into the air.

LIFE-BOAT.

"A whale, sartin! Don't I wish I was nearer and had a good harpoon in my hand?"

A GREENLAND WHALE.

They went no nearer though, for the steamer went on its way sending up a column of black smoke, and the whale as if in emulation sent up a jet of foaming water and then pushed on his way.

"Oh, Mr. Bobstay, do tell us about whales?" asked Ralph.

"Do you wish me to?" replied the old salt with a complacent grin. "Well, I guess I will, some of these fine days."

But all through the steamer's voyage, that "some day" did not arrive. Either Jack was busy, or Siah was needed at the furnaces, or Ralph and Rick could not come at the appointed hour.

HOW MANY WAVES THERE SEEMED TO BE!

Meantime, the ocean behind them was growing bigger and the ocean before them was growing smaller. The steamer's engines ceaselessly panted night and day. The great hull kept rising and falling with the sea, yet ever going forward, and the Land of the Sunrise, so long a dream, promised soon to become a fact before the pilgrims' eyes. "Every wave takes us nearer," said Ralph; but how many waves there seemed to be!

SHIP AHOY!—

CHAPTER VIII.

SUNRISE LAND AT LAST.

FUJISAN, THE HIGHEST MOUNTAIN IN JAPAN.

PATIENT-ly did the engine of the steamer toil away, and every minute, Rick and Ralph were coming nearer to the Sunrise Land.

"We have been out so many days that we have gone between four and five thousand miles, and to-morrow we ought to see Yokohama," said Jack Bobstay.

"And all this, time," moaned Ralph, "I have not seen the sun rise."

"Haven't you? Come on deck to-morrow morning early and see it."

That evening, Uncle Nat and his nephews watched the sun go down into the sea. They saw him floating a moment upon the water, and then gradually sinking like an immense coal of fire.

"There, boys, the sun looks pretty big, but if we could stand upon the planet Venus, he would appear larger still."

"Why?" asked Rick.

"Because Venus is nearer to the sun."

"And I have studied at school that from Mercury the sun must be vastly more huge."

"Yes, Ralph, because Mercury is still nearer the sun, and so merged in the glory of the sun, that without a telescope it is no easy thing finding Mercury. The great astronomer Copernicus never saw Mercury, though it is true he had no telescope. While the sun appears so big from Mercury, from the farthest planets he must shrink to a very humble size."

Uncle Nat, when in his state-

room, showed the boys the accompanying picture of the different sizes of the sun when viewed from different planets.

Ralph declared that " the sun, big as a ginger-snap when seen from Mercury, was only a pin-head from Neptune."

Ralph was out of his bed at an early hour, the next morning, and came upon deck rubbing his eyes.

" Ho, there you are ! " sang out Jack Bobstay. " Have you got your sea-legs on ? You may find the deck wet and slippery, for we had a heavy dew or something else last night."

Ralph turned to the east. It was very early and the clouds were just beginning to light up. Between the steamer and the horizon, the sea was one vast surface of jet, as if a fire had gone over and blackened this prairie-like area and had then been swept beyond the rim of the sea into a deep, deep furnace that shot a warm glow up among the clouds. Ralph came again in a little while. The east was full of sharper light, the clouds stretching one above another in gold and red and orange strata, while higher up swept and towered broken, fugitive masses of mist, like smoke from a vast prairie-fire. The sea had now brightened from black to gray, and stretched toward the east like a great ashy hearth. But where was the fire itself ? Was it still beneath the sea sending up that sharp, intense light, every moment burning sharper and intenser ? Suddenly, away over on the edge of this hearth, appeared a bright, shining little coal ! How pure and golden !

" But it grows ! " said Ralph.

Yes, this tip of a fire-brand steadily enlarged, flashing, sparkling dazzling, till it hung a huge ball of fire above the sea, and thousands of little waves stirred and glittered as if consciously to lift and offer some crown to this king of the day.

" Ain't she a beauty ? " said Jack Bobstay looking silently over Ralph's shoulder and watching the same scene. " Now turn and look westward ! "

Ralph swung round and what did·he see? On the edge of the sea was a glorious pyramid of snow. Was the earth rising up to do early honor to this king of gold, and holding up a fair, white crown for his wearing?

"What is that?" asked Ralph in tones of surprise and admiration.

"That is a famous mountain on this side of the Pacific," said Jack gently patting Ralph's shoulder, "grand old Fujisan, and it is the pride of all Japan."

"Then we are near Japan?"

"Sartin'. Run and tell Boson."

Ralph hurried away and speedily brought Rick who finished dressing himself as he came along. The two boys were in ecstasy.

"Let's have Uncle Nat up," said Rick.

Uncle Nat was forced to leave his warm nest and come up to see the sights. One excellent thing about Uncle Nat was, that he could enter thoroughly into a boy's feelings, and he said "My!" and "Pshaw!" and "Look-er-there!" as many times as his enthusiastic nephews desired.

"It will take us some time yet to get to harbor, boys, for you can see old Fuji some way off."

"But we shall get there to-day. We are coming, Sunrise Land!" said Ralph.

And the steamer's engines groaning all the way across the Pacific, now seemed.to change their tune, and said with every piston-stroke, "Com‑ing! com‑ing! com‑ing, Sun‑rise Land!"

At last Jack Bobstay could say to the boys, "We are passing Cape King, and that is at the entrance of the bay leading to Yokohama."

"And is it Japan on both sides of us?" asked Rick, eagerly looking around.

"Yes, Boson. We are going by the pint, and there is the light-house. We are about a dozen miles from Yokohama. There is a big city, Tokiyo, the capital, up the bay."

A VIEW IN TOKIYO.

The morning breeze went like a broom over the bay, stirring it into little ripples. Now and then the steamer rushed by an island, and again it shot past an odd-looking Japanese junk. This was very high in the stern, but low in the bows, and carried wide sails swollen by the wind. Sometimes these sails were made of matting or bamboo. Amidships, it looked as if a house with a pitch bamboo-roof had been built. The cargo was stored uuder this roof. Rick saw birds skimming the waters of the bay, and at a distance the birds and the junks resembled one another. Vessels were passed, at whose mastheads floated the colors of European nations. There were steamers from Shanghai, steamers from Marseilles, steamers from Hong Kong, steamers from Southampton. There were store-ships too, and coal-hulks. Back of the shipping in the harbor, were the tiled roofs of Yokohama and still farther in the rear was a swell of land called the Bluff, and dotted with houses. The Bluff is a quarter occupied with many handsome residences of Europeans especially. Outside of all, rose the hills, swelling like waves from the sea that did not know when and where to stop, but continued to roll back from the shore till petrified by some resistless edict.

At Yokohama, there were no wharves, and consequently the passengers were dependent on boats for transportation. Boats were not wanting, by any means. The moment the steamer let go her anchor, she became a target at which boats began to shoot from every quarter. Their occupants were muscular men, and had stout arms well-adapted to their work.

"They look queer," thought Ralph. "They have a dingy yellow skin, and my! their heads are shaven in the middle, and a top-knot sticks up."

Ralph watched the Japanese boatmen as they sculled their boats rapidly along. The oar they used was in two parts, securely fastened together. Resting on the gunwale of the boat, this oar is held there by a pin, and then worked as in sculling, the sweep at the handle of the oar being about two feet. Ralph heard one singing as he sculled.

"O see them scull, Rick!" cried Ralph.

The scullers were lively enough, writhing away till they reached the steamer, and then they did not use the muscles of their arms but their mouths, yelling away as enthusiastically as the starter of an American horse-car at a railway station. Some of the steamer's passengers were preparing to go ashore, and among these was our party. Rick had taken a sorrowful leave of Siah and Jack Bobstay, but he had not yet said good-bye to Joe Pigtail, and was it strange if he found it hard to part from pretty Amy Clarendon, a little girl whose acquaintance he had made on board the steamer? This last agony struck deep into Rick's tender heart.

"Good-bye all," said Uncle Nat hurrying off, and then he added in his cheery way, "may we meet again! Come, boys, come!"

"Me see you again, may be!" exclaimed Joe.

Amy Clarendon was waving her hand, and Rick thought she never looked prettier. The stoical Ralph had said his good-byes, and went off promptly, but Rick moved with hesitating steps, for his heart was full. He must have one more look at — Joe — Pigtail, and he fell behind Uncle Nat and Ralph. Allowing his eyes to rest on Amy's sweet face, he was saying, "God — bless — dear — Joe — "

"Look here, youngster, hurry along! My valise almost went down your throat then," said a passenger who had a very disagreeable, jerky style of speech Rick thought. "Let 'dear Joe' go and move on, please!"

Rick moved on, but with a breaking heart.

The next morning, Uncle Nat happened to see under Rick's pillow these lines of newspaper poetry, and as he rather liked poetry he began to read the first stanza:

> "How oft, alas! thy charming face,
>   Will shine athwart my dreams!
> In such a moment, darkest night
>   Like brightest moon-day seems."

"That will do!" said Uncle Nat — "Nonsense! A bad case of the measles!"

Measles! It was something far more romantic, for Rick's pillow-companion had sent him, the night before, into dream-land, and there he and somebody else wandered away 'mid groves and flowers and birds and streams and — so forth.

CHAPTER IX.

IN YOKOHAMA.

A STYLE OF DRESS.

"WA! ho! ho! huida!"

What was that? It was a strange, dismal sound that came to Ralph and Rick as they went with Uncle Nat into the Japanese quarter of Yokohama. In the foreign section, there were features reminding them of home. There were handsome stores with fine stone-fronts. There were hotels and banks. There were street-lamps. Foreigners abounded.

In the native quarter of Yokohama, one saw sights and heard sounds peculiarly Japanese. The place abounded in novelties. And now up from the street came this low, hoarse cry, "Wa! ho! ho! huida!" It was a series of groans and grunts. Stepping out doors, they saw a native cart well loaded with bales of goods. The cart had two wheels, and the motive power was not that of horses but men. Between the shafts and at the same time behind a cross-bar, two men were propelling. Then at the rear of the cart were two more men steadily shoving. All four were humped and bowed as if working prodigiously, and lost to everything but the occupation of cart-shoving, but whoever did the shoving, the two men in front were dismally groaning, and those behind replied, and a grunting time they had of it. There were many of these man-carts in the streets, conveying goods. There was a scarcity of horse-flesh, and the boys missed the clattering of hoofs, and also the rumbling of heavy carts making Boston-streets so noisy.

Ralph went back to his room at the International Hotel, saying he must look up something on Japan. Throwing himself back on a comfortable sofa, he began to read a book that Uncle Nat gave him. When Ralph and Rick reached Concord again, they arranged for a lecture on Japan in their barn. Rick took the tickets, five cents for adults, two cents for boys of ten, and half of the latter price for still younger children. Three empty soap-boxes piled one upon the other made a lecturer's table whose height of four feet was about as ambitious as would accommodate the lecturer, and behind his barricade

ON A COMFORTABLE SOFA.

stood Ralph reading from a manuscript. A barn-lantern suspended from the roof shed a very, very thin light upon the audience, and gave the lecturer only a tenth of a chance to read his manuscript. The audience consisted of Gus Freeman, Joe Simes, Tom Eaton and Billy Blaney, who for the consideration of two cents had been admitted to "an exhibition of Japanese Curiosities, also a Performance of Japanese feats, to be preceded by a lecture from Ralph Rogers, Esq., recently from Japan." Gus Freeman as an intimate friend was passed in free, a dead-head. This entertainment had been advertised on posters as extensively as the surface of the garden-gate would permit. A portion of what Ralph said that afternoon came from his reading on the sofa in the International Hotel, and other items he gathered through those faithful gleaners, the eyes and ears.   As Bridget Mahoney,

STREET IN YOKOHAMA.

the servant, put up her head above the barn-chamber stairs, at Mrs. Rogers' request, to see what was going on, it enabled Ralph to say,

"*Ladies and Gentlemen:* — Japan is a very interesting place. It is, as has been said, our next-door western neighbor, that is of any special size. It is well therefore for us who are young men to-day," (applause from Gus, Joe, Tom, and Billy,) "to get some idea on the subject.   Japan is a spot in the temperate zone, or spots rather, for it is an empire of islands, the principal being Hondo, Kiushiu, Yezo and Shikoku.   It is claimed to have three thousand eight hundred islands in all.   Put all its miles together and they would not make a country equal to France, which our republic can swallow at least fifteen times.

"The people number about thirty-five millions, and are quite bright, and in some things cannot be beat, even by a Concord-boy. (Applause.) Every country has its savage wild people, who are thought to be the first settlers. These in Japan are the Ainos. They live in houses that are made of reeds fastened upon a wooden frame-work, and these have a sharp, high roof. The ridge-pole is decorated. The people are inferior to the Japanese. Japan is quite mountianous, and has a bad way of shaking sometimes, but the people do not seem to mind it. There are hundreds of dead volcanoes, and over twenty are still alive and kicking. The crack mountain of Japan is Fujisan, which is about thirteen thousand feet above the ocean, and for a hundred miles away can be seen. For nine months at least in the year, its peaked top is covered with snow. The Japanese have a map of twelve provinces from which it can be seen. The people hold it in sacred awe, and travel hundreds of miles that they may reach its top and there worship. If any of my audience should honor Japan with a visit, they will see Fujisan as they near the coast, and it is a very handsome sight, as my companion, the Hon. Richard Rogers, will testify. (The Hon. Richard Rogers about this time was staining his face that he might take the part of a Japanese juggler in the coming feats.) The Japanese are very nice workmen in fancy goods, and they get up some cunning things in gardening, like dwarf trees and plants. They are introducing American and European ideas, and in some places are adopting them quite rapidly.

"The old-style Japanese dress is a kind of gown or long frock called the kimono, and around the waist goes a girdle or sash, the women wearing it broader than the men, and the ends the ladies tie behind as a bustle. Besides the kimono, a shorter garment is often worn over it called the haori. Many of the men, the younger ones, wear hakama or big trousers over the kimono, letting the haori stay outside. The women like to fix up their hair in bows and bunches, and go bare-headed. The girdle is a very convenient place to stow away things in, and the sleeves in the Japanese dress are so big that they become famous store-houses. The aristocracy afford themselves silk, but the lower classes have plainer stuff like calico and linen.

"There was a class of troublesome nobles called the daimiyo, that have now been set aside. Their old court dress must have given them a look like a full-blown snap-dragon, and I guess the government found them all that. The

new-style dress is the foreign one of coat and pants, and is coming into use pretty fast in some places. You will see government officers wearing it, and it is the fashionable evening dress, but some people don't look as if they felt at home in it. The emperor rides out in a European carriage, and dresses in the European style. The houses are apt to be rather low and they build them of wood generally. But in some places like Yoko-hama, they are beginning to build more solid." (Here Gus and Billy be-gan to be drowsy, as the auditorium was rather "close," and Ralph re-sorted to a ruse. "Fire! Fire!" he shouted. Billy and Gus started, and be-gan to gaze about wildly)

DAIMIYO IN COURT DRESS.

"I was only going to remark,' resumed the lecturer, "that they have had some fearful fires in Japan, because the houses are so generally of wood and so lightly built, but as I said they are building more solid. The head of the Japanese gov.

THE WAY THE MIKADO TRAVELLED IN JAPANESE FASHION.

ernment is the Mikado, and he has an army and navy, into both of which foreign ideas have made their way. The Japanese flag is a red sun on a white ground. The climate is what you might expect in the temperate zone. They have winds that blow pretty hard and come pretty quick. Around Yokohama, the snow is seldom seen deeper than two or three inches, but then there are other places where it comes heavier, sometimes in mountain-valleys accumulating to a great depth, and I think I could stand a little more than they have at Yokohama."

If the eloquent lecturer had said, " a little more light," it would have been more appropriate. The barn-chandelier threatened to fail the lecturer, as the light began to sputter. It soon shamefully went out altogether, leaving Ralph in a predicament. At first, he attempted to extemporize, but in a moment he was ominously pausing and " hem-hemming." He saved himself however by fiercely declaring that he would rather live in old Concord than in Yokohama, for on the hills at home, winter did give a boy a good chance to coast. Giving way now to a " noted Japanese juggler," the lecturer was rewarded by the enthusiastic applause of the audience for this compliment to New England coasting.

CHAPTER X.

EARTHQUAKES AND RAILROADS.

RECONNIOTERING FOR AN EARTHQUAKE.

RICK awoke the next night and was startled to find himself trembling. Was the trembling inside of him or outside of him? He could hardly determine the point. The agitation came again. Still more thoroughly frightened now, he was conscious that while his heart within was thumping, the bed without was shaking.

"Ralph!" exclaimed Rick in a hoarse whisper.

No answer.

"Ralph!" Another shaking; floor, walls, furniture — all trembling. Had the evil spirits of the Japanese come into the house?

The sleeper stirred and said, "What is it?"

"Did you hear that, Ralph?"

"No — Yes."

"Something awful. Let's get out of bed and speak to Uncle Nat."

They both sprang out of bed and started for "dear Uncle Nat," as Rick said in his heart, dearer now than ever.

" Uncle Nat ! "

No reply but a snore.

At Uncle Nat's bedside, there stood in the moonlight, two trembling boys, each face colorless as a sheet.

" Uncle Nat ! " called Rick. " Uncle Nat ! "

His sleepy relative groaned.

" Did you hear that ? "

" Y — e — s — "

" What was it ? "

" You — hol — ler — ing."

" No, but the shaking."

" Oh — it's Yo — yo — ko — "

" Yokohama ? "

" Yes, she's — got — the shakes."

" Got what ? "

" A fit — of ag — ag — ue."

" What ? "

" Earthquake, child ! go to bed."

" Oh uncle ! "

Rick almost expected to see a great mouth yawning beneath him, swallowing him and Ralph up. No mouth opened. But what was that noise ? It was Uncle Nat snoring again. Plainly, he was not afraid. The brothers went to the windows and looked out.

" Let's see if we can see anything," said Ralph in a hushed voice.

No earthquake was visible, nor was any disturbance anywhere manifest. The white moonlight rested like a fresh fall of snow on all the house-roofs. The boys crept back to bed, and cuddled down beside one another, directing two sober faces and four big eyes toward the moonlight. A late comer was heard to open the hotel door, then his footsteps sounded on the stairs, and finally the boys caught the rattling of a key·in the lock of an adjoining door. All was now still. Ralph fell asleep. Two eyes were left staring at the moonlight, but Rick began to be drowsy and one eye ceased its watch. At last the snowy moonlight was searching everywhere, but not an eye was open to follow its progress over the floor.

The next morning, Rick said to Uncle Nat: "Were not you afraid?"

THE ROUND MOON.

"Afraid? No, they have earthquakes too often for that."

"But don't they do harm Uncle Nat?"

"Well, yes, sometimes; I heard a man at the breakfast table say that years ago, there was a very malicious earthquake. It shook and shook and shook, and it brought down heavy roofs of tiles, and sixty thousand people were crushed to death. I understand there was a heavy one recently, a great chimney-tumbler. There are generally three shocks and the second is the worst."

The next night, the earthquake came again. Uncle Nat in the meantime had changed his room, and when Ralph and Rick, aroused by the shock, left their bed to slip on their clothes and hunt for Uncle Nat in his new quarters, they stole along the entry guided by the moonlight, only to find and enter — whose room? ·

THE MIKADO ON A JOURNEY IN EUROPEAN FASHION.

"Oh Uncle Nat, she's come again!"

"Another earthquake, Uncle Nat! It's me and Rick," said Ralph.

The two boys were pressing into the room half-lighted by the moon-beams, when out of the curtains enclosing a bed, the face of an old man was protruded, a long scalp-lock and a sharp nose projecting into the light that the round moon at the window shed so liberally.

"Show, show!" said a thin querulous voice. "Little boys musn't be up making a noise at this time of night. You must go right to your room. Now go!"

And they went.

Rogers brothers thought they would rather live in New England even if there they could not get some things the Japanese had. But by nine o'clock, the next morning, the subject of earthquakes was entirely forgotten, as the boys were full of anticipation of a railroad ride from Yokohama to Tokiyo, the capital.

"Will not Dr. Walton go with us?" asked the boys.

"I guess so," replied Uncle Nat. "We might ask him."

Dr. Walton was a physician from Boston, who had been in Japan a number of years. Boarding at the International, he had made the acquaintance of Uncle Nat and his nephews. The boys took to him decidedly. He was about thirty, rather tall and rather stout. His complexion was very clear, taking on a blush almost as readily as a baby's, and his eyes were like handsome black cherries.

"Yes, I do like Dr. Walton," declared Ralph.

"And so do I," responded Rick.

When dressing for an evening walk, the doctor threw over his shoulders a student's cloak whose folds drooped with a peculiar grace, the boys' admiration was enthusiastic. It was then they thought they would rather stroll with him than with the mikado himself. When Dr. Walton said he would go to Tokiyo with them, they knew that on account of his long Japanese residence he would make a valuable companion. The party took the cars at the fine railroad station of stone in Yokohama. Everything was now ready, and the engine commencing to spit and cough as if to get cinders out of its throat, the cars rumbled away.

"Oh see," said Ralph looking out of a car-window, there's a —"

"Jinrikisha," said the doctor.

"Jim Ricker's Shay?" asked Rick. "Who's he?'

"It isn't a boy — it's a carriage," said Ralph chagrined at the younger Rogers' ignorance of Japanese facts.

"A jinrikisha is for riding purposes, and it always seemed to me like an American baby carriage. One man draws, and another pushes behind, when a long distance is to be travelled, but in short journeys a single man draws. It goes faster than a baby carriage, I can assure you, for the men propelling it are strong fellows. You can travel forty miles a day, and more even in the jinrikisha—style. One day, I went seventy-two miles, riding from five in the morning to seven at night, changing men. The jinrikisha moves at about the rate of an American horse-car. We rely on them a good deal for riding purposes, and while there are hundreds of jinrikishas in Yokohama, in Tokiyo there are thousands. It is cheap riding, only two cents for a short distance; and for ten cents you can keep your jinrikisha an hour, and for fifty cents all day. The motion in this carriage is a little peculiar, but you get used to it."

After this statement by the doctor, Rick made up his mind it must be splendid to ride in "Jim Ricker's Shay" and resolved to try it at the first opportunity that offered.

Looking out of the car-windows again, they saw a cart in a road near by. The cart was heaped high with vegetables. In front, pulled a man, and behind the cart was a woman who pushed with docility.

The vehicle halted, and the man and his female-assistant stared at the passing, rattling train.

" There, don't you suppose they envy us, doctor ? "

" Yes, captain, and perhaps they hate the foreign innovation. When the telegraph wires were put up, the farmers were so hostile that when one was stretched over their fields, they said the evil spirits would not favor their crops, and they — not the evil spirits but the farmers, though the latter acted like them — cut the wire and then tried to smash the glass insulators of the poles ! It was a mystery to them how a message could go over the wire, and they would watch curiously a long while to see the news travel ! When this railroad was opened less than ten years ago, I was present. They had a big time, and the big officials including the *mikado*, or emperor, were present. One very marked thing was the presenting of an address to the emperor by a deputation of four merchants. That was a great thing in Japan, when the merchant-caste, which does not stand high, thus approached and saw the mikado, a being once bottled up and kept in the dark, so to speak, like phosphorus."

" What is that man doing ? " asked Ralph calling the doctor's attention to a person who seemed to be stopping at the side of a road they passed. The stranger was intent on work he held in his lap.

" That must be an artist," answered the doctor, " and he seems to be sketching something. The Japanese, you know, are very fond of drawing and painting. Some of their sketches are ugly and grotesque, but very original certainly. And they show genius of a certain kind. Here is a horse," and the doctor showed a picture he had with him. " This horse certainly is full of fire and yet the artist executing it did it in seven strokes, adding a few brush-sweeps for tail and mane. The Japanese have peculiar skill in outline drawing. They will dash off the form of a bird, and the whole thing is very spirited."

CHAPTER XI.

SIGHT-SEEING IN TOKIYO.

TOKIYO, the capital of Japan, interested the boys very much, and in the company of Uncle Nat and the doctor, they started out to see what they could find.

"What is this street?" asked the inquisitive Rick.

"This is the Tori, a prominent street in the capital. You see how many people are here. All sorts of craft sail into these quarters," answered the doctor.

Rick was interested in the conveyances there. There were the man-carts for mer-

THE SEVEN-STROKED HORSE. (*See page* 117.)

chandise, the jinrikishas for passengers, and there was the kago, a vehicle that offered foot-sore pedestrians a ride if they would get into a covered basket suspended from a pole borne on men's shoulders, but this last vehicle is one seldom seen in Tokiyo. There was a great, busy throng in the street, and side by side walked Old Japan and New Japan. There were those still clinging to the Japanese dress, and some that wore the coat and pants fashionable beyond the seas. There were police who like American police wore uniforms. A horse and carriage went past the boys. And the shops, who could count them? Their style was peculiar, their roofs being heavily covered with black tiles. Where these tiles were jointed, they showed narrow white strips of mortar.

"O see, Uncle Nat," cried Rick. "See that man selling goods."

It was a Japanese not actually selling to a purchaser, but waiting for one. He sat on a floor that had been covered with matting, and on either side were piles of his goods offered for every one's inspection, the front of the store having been entirely removed.

"If you would like," said the doctor, "we will look at some of the streets about here. You will find special lines of goods in those we visit, and the array is interesting. Let us go to the Dyers' street."

Here were dyed goods, and one readily detected the odor of the vats for the immersing of articles to be colored. In another street there was nothing but bureaus and cabinets.

"See," said Ralph, "there's a man sawing and he pulls the saw toward him rather than pushes it from him as we do."

"The teeth are not set the same way as ours but the reverse," replied the doctor.

In a third street, they found goods that had come across the seas.

"The old beer bottles!" exclaimed Rick who was a total abstinence boy. "Must these things come over too?"

They went into Bamboo street where the shop-keepers sold bamboo poles. One street the boys called pretty, as folding screens were there, and upon these, pictures had been sketched and poetry written.

"We have plenty of streets in Tokiyo," said the doctor. "Some are named after the occupations of the people in them, such as

Blacksmith and Cooper. There are those named after trees or flowers like Cedar and Chrysanthemum. Plum Orchard street may be found, also Wheat and Indigo streets. There are those having fanciful names like 'Abounding Gladness.'"

They had been looking at the signs displayed by different stores. A goldbeater announced his presence by huge spectacles, substituting gold for glass. The kite-maker was advertised by a cuttle-fish, and a trader in cut flowers showed the sign of a little willow tree. Every spiked white ball — and these would average eighteen inches in diameter — threw the boys into a pleasureable excitement, for the white ball meant a candy shop. Still strolling about, Ralph suddenly exclaimed, "There is water, doctor!"

"Yes, that is a canal, very handy in carrying goods about, and we have many canals in Tokiyo."

"Couldn't we have a boat-ride, Uncle Nat?"

"Oh yes, I would like to have a ride myself. Here, here. Take us round, won't you?" said Uncle Nat, calling to a boatman who brought his craft to the bank at once. "Don't you see, boys, how he understood me. Either I talk good Japanese, or he knows good English. Step aboard!"

The craft was one that carried what the boys called "a cunning cabin," a little house in the centre, and through its windows they could look and see what was passing, as the boatman polled it along. There were the skiffs of fruit sellers, and boats loaded with merchandise, or fishermen sculled along their crafts while boys on the banks took their first lesson in the piscatory art, and into the canal dropped their lines "for a bite."

"We go at a pretty good rate, don't we, Rick? Almost as fast as you did, last summer, when you tried to make that boat go," said Ralph.

NIHON BASHI.

121

"What was that, Rick?" inquired Uncle Nat.

Rick was blushing. He did not recall that exploit with satisfaction, for it was one day when deeply in love with a very young lady at a summer resort, he attempted to give her a boat-ride on an adjacent pond, and in his excitement had forgotten to untie the rope!

Ralph very kindly spared the champion oarsman any further mortification, and the subject was dropped.

Another day, they went to the famous Nihon Bashi, a bridge, and from it looked off upon the tiled roofs of the city and upon the snowy cone of Fugisan. Before them, too, were the towers of the famous castle of Tokiyo. This castle was also visited. They saw its walls of stone, the deep, wide moats without, extending eleven miles in all. That day, one other

THE CHAMPION OARSMAN.

noteworthy place was reached, a palace belonging to the emperor. Beautiful grounds measuring a hundred acres adjoined this palace.

"This is a big place," observed Uncle Nat "this city of Tokiyo."

"Yes, captain, and so the old emperor Iyeyasu was right when he believed the city would be something, and in making bounds for Tokiyo, he went far beyond the settled quarters and set up towers and gates without any connecting walls, believing that some day they would be erected. People laughed at his work, but he was right. We have seen to-day some of the better parts of the city. This will do for to-day, I guess."

"No," thought Rick, "it won't do. I have not ridden in a 'Jim

GRANDPA'S CLOCK.

Ricker's Shay' yet. I will, if Uncle Nat lets me, this very day."

That afternoon, while Uncle Nat and the doctor were away, Rick and Ralph were in their room at the hotel.

"I wonder what time it is, Ralph."

"I don't know, Rick, for we have no clock."

"Oh dear," sighed the younger brother in his heart. "I wish a clock was as handy here as at grandpa's."

That clock at grandpa's, how Rick when younger would watch it! But he was thousands of miles away from grandpa's and nothing like a clock was in the room. He went down to the hotel office to learn the hour. Passing the outer door, he looked through and saw a jinrikisha waiting by the sidewalk. Its runners wore big bowl-like hats, and were dressed in blue shirts and blue tights. A thought came to him ; why not take this jinrikisha and go down to that store where Uncle Nat and the doctor said they were going ?

"The shopkeeper's name is Inu and I can write it, I guess," con-.cluded Rick.

Uncle Nat, however, had not said that the man's name was Inu. Rick had asked for it, and Uncle Nat answered, "I knew, but " — That moment he was called out of the room. Rick caught the "I knew," he did not hear the "but."

"Ah," thought Rick, "it is Inu, which is a Japanese word."

It happens that the word means "dog."

Uncle Nat had told the boys to pick up all the knowledge they could, and they had been practicing on a few Japanese words and Rick could write "Inu." He put "Inu" on a slip of paper, pointed in the supposed direction of the shop, and as he handed the slip to the bearers, with a lordly air mounted the jinrikisha. The men took the paper, read it and threw it away. Then they turned to Rick, smiled affectionately, and trotted off with their princely burden. One runner would have been enough, but Rick meant to go in a style as ostentatious as possible.

"How intelligent the Japanese are," said Rick, "and, what a good knowledge I have of the language. I shouldn't wonder if I could find my way all over Japan myself without Uncle Nat and the doctor. Nice, knowing people, these Japanese."

The men had said to one another, "Inu! It means that he has lost a dog and wants us to find it. We will do what we can." Away they went.

He soon noticed that they stopped and made inquiries, a fact which he could not understand, for he supposed that every one knew where "Mr. Inu" kept. The men wheeled into various streets, occasionally halting and apparently asking questions.

"Look here!" Rick shouted. "Why don't you go to Mr. Inu's?" The men smiled blandly and nodding went on. Once they stopped and patting a dog, made signs to Rick. He was in disgust.

"Lazy fellers!" he bawled. "Don't stop to fool with that dog. You don't half earn your money. Don't you know Mr. Inu's place?"

"It is not his dog and we must hunt farther," they said and still smiling they trundled forward their small load of a volcano.

Rick was now furious.

"It is I – nu, I – nu! Must I spell it, I – n – u! Don't you understand, boobies?"

On they went, stopping now and then to speak to people. Rick thought to himself, "How hateful these men do look!" The day was quite warm for spring, and these intelligent Japanese had laid aside their hats, and their half-bald heads went bobbing up and down like gooseberries rolling over pebbles. Rick thought of Charley Ross, the Philadelphia boy, and conjectured that these men must have been poor Charley's kidnappers, and what if they should kidnap him too!

"Stop!' he yelled.

The men now were not so smiling, for they were tired of the game. They again stopped, and began to jabber away at Rick like parrots. He in his turn was thoroughly vexed, and was spitting out his anger at them. He began to doubt whether it would be so easy to get through Japan if all the people were such boors as these, and how he longed for Uncle Nat. A crowd had now collected, and things looked squally.

In the mean time, Uncle Nat and the doctor had returned to the hotel and there were inquiries at once made for the missing Rick. A servant reported that Rick had been seen in a jinrikisha moving off from the hotel-door.

"Moving off?" repeated Uncle Nat. "I guess it is time for me to move off also, and hunt up that young traveller."

The doctor offered to accompany him. They hunted and hunted but in vain. At last, they saw in the street a crowd, and in the midst of this, was the lost Rick, screaming away at his runners, they heartily screaming back.

"Ship ahoy!" shouted Uncle, Nat making his way through the crowd. Glad enough was Rick to bring his independent travels in Japan to an end and return to the hotel with Uncle Nat. He tried to tell his uncle how it had happened, but Uncle Nat was greatly puzzled to understand the course of his remarks.

"Look here, young man," said Uncle Nat, "the next time you want to make a trip, you had better know just where you are going, how you are going, and if you don't get there, whether you can get back."

Rick thought so too.

The next day they all went to a noted spot in Tokiyo, Asakusa.

"Why it looks like Boston Common on the Fourth of July," said Ralph. They had reached rows of booths making a showy display of goods. There were shops too for the sale of toys, of ladies' hair pins, and smokers' comforts. Then came booths where one could buy little idols or amulet bags or incense burners. This showed they were nearing the more sacred part of Asakusa. When they reached the temple, they found a motley collection of idols, some of the figures being hideous. There were gardens too in which grew the azalea, camellia, lotus and chrysanthemum.

Everywhere were people. Some were trading at the tobacco booths, or drinking out of little cups at the tea-booths. There were men saying their prayers before the temple-shrines, and robed priests were bowing in their services. It was a queer mixture to the boys, "a great gala day," as Ralph said, "and some praying thrown in."

PAGAN TEMPLE IN JAPAN.

"Oh, see that," exclaimed Rick.

Before Binzuru, a medicine-deity, was a girl who rubbed a leg of the god and then her own.

"That means," said the doctor, "that she has hurt her leg, and is transferring virtue from the god to her limb. For generations they have rubbed the poor god so much that his face is decidedly worn. Nose and ears, you see, have all gone."

The travellers that day saw also Shiba, a collection of temples and tombs. In Shiba sleep some of the old Japanese shoguns or military rulers: a famous resting-place of the dead.

That night the doctor showed the boys a picture of the god of Longevity

A SINTOO GOD — THE GOD OF LONGEVITY.

"You see he is riding contentedly on a stork, and the stork is very calmly sailing above a flood."

"I should think, doctor," said Ralph, "he would scare the life out of a man, rather than put life into him."

JAPANESE SHOPS.

CHAPTER XII.

"DON'T you think, doctor, that the Japanese people are funny, to have so many fans?" asked Rick, running in from the street.

"It might seem so, but then " — here the doctor looked at the little fellow who was trying to carry a quantity of fans in his hand — "but then somebody else seems to like fans also. Where did you get so many?"

"Oh, I picked 'em up in the street. Some I bought, you know, for they are so cheap. I am going to give them away to my friends."

Here Rick arranged them in order, as shown in the illustration.

"There, that first one, a sort of half-round one, is for Aunt Mary; the next, that opens and shuts, is for mother; the round one is for Nurse Fennel, and those three others are for my three cousins — Aunt Mary's girls. The one with the long handle is Uncle Thomas', because — because he has short arms, but a long neck, and has some way to reach up. The little one at the bottom is for a baby in the next house."

"But, Rick, you have not disposed of all the fans."

Rick blushed. He had kept one for Amy Clarendon, if he ever met that beloved object.

"Why, doctor," said Rick, anxious to change the subject, "I saw a man giving a piece of money to a beggar, and he put it on a fan."

"And I heard of a poor fellow of pretty high rank who was sentenced to death, and his fate announced to him by presenting him with a fan. There are all sorts of fans, as you will find out. The other day, I was pretty warm, and a gentleman, at whose house I called, handed me a fan that you could dip in water. Its material was waterproof, and the water on the fan as it evaporated would cool the breeze it wafted upon you. You will find all kinds of pictures on fans, and various inscriptions, also. Some are very pretty and ingenious. A great man may stick his autograph on a fan. Here in Tokiyo, they make some elegant fans."

"Don't you think Japanese artists are queer? I mean, they have an odd way of painting."

"It seems to us so, Rick. They have an appreciative sense of what is funny; and then, they rather enjoy the horrible. It is worth while to notice some things on fans, for they are emblematic. You are apt to see on fans the bamboo and sparrow, or the willow and swallow, and these are signs of domestic

YOUNG AMERICA BEHIND A JAPANESE FENCE.

happiness. As for the matter of emblems, it is worth while to notice those on all kinds of articles. Sometimes, certainly, they are very significant and appropriate. For instance: When a little gown is given to a baby, you will be likely to see on it the pine-tree and stork. These mean long life.

"The stork is a favorite bird in Japan; and when it comes to art they love to reproduce the bird, with his long legs and long bill."

It was Ralph's turn the next day to bring in something curious, and his article was a dwarf tree, given to Uncle Nat by a friend. It was growing in a small pot, and for a pigmy, it looked very vigorous. .

"That is a pine tree, Ralph."

"A pine?"

"Yes; the Japanese are wonderful gardeners, and while we at home like to see how big a flower we can get, they delight most in seeing how little a thing they can produce. They like to raise pines only a few inches high. And then, they like to bring their growing things into all kinds of

shapes. You may see a vegetable cat staring at you out of
the evergreen you notice; or, it may be a European wearing a
hat, and wrought out of the same material. You may see hens, or a
rooster, or a Japanese junk under full sail. They trim, also, the larch
in this way. One flower, that is a kind of national blossom, is the
chrysanthemum. It is adopted as the Emperor's crest, and it
appears about government offices. Flowers are exceedingly popular,
and in every house they try to have flowers on New Year's day.
When the plum blossoms in February or early March, the cherry
in April, the lotus in July, the chrysanthemum in autumn, and the
camellia in winter, there are multitudes of admirers ready to appreciate
these beauties. With certain kinds of blooms are sure to come excursions of the Japanese, to rejoice over them."

Uncle Nat heard the conversation between the doctor and his nephew,
and pulling out his pocket-book, he said: "Perhaps, doctor, you will be
so kind as to tell me the meaning of these pictures, which I found
on some bank-bills."

The doctor took up the bills and remarked: "The Japanese are
very proud of their history and love to preserve it in their sketches.
Here is a bank-bill modeled after our American bank-bills, and this
picture has an interesting story connected with it. Over five hundred
years ago Go Daigo was emperor. There was an opposition to him,
and falling before it he was sentenced to banishment. On his way
to exile, a young nobleman, Kojima Takanori, tried to rescue his sovereign; but, mistaking the road, he and his followers were too late to
accomplish their purpose. His followers would not go farther with
him, but he determined to proceed alone. For several days he tried
to reach the sovereign's side, and say in private some word of hope;
but the emperor was so closely guarded, there was no chance to bring
this about. Kojima then thought of this stratagem. Stealing into

OUR JAPANESE LUXURIES ON A HOT AUGUST DAY.

the garden connected with the quarters where the emperor's jailers were passing the night, Kojima found a cherry tree. Scraping off its bark he wrote on the white surface inside two lines, which, translated, mean:

Oh Heaven, destroy not Kosen
While Hanrei still lives!

"The emperor's guard the next morning saw the scraped tree and the characters there, and wondered what had happened; but it was a fortunate thing for the emperor that they could not read the lines. They showed them to him, and he saw the meaning at once. The reference was to Kosen, a Chinese king, who, cast down from his throne, was elevated again by a faithful vassal, Hanrei. The significance of it was at once appreciated, and Go Daigo was secretly comforted. He knew that he could not be friendless; and Kojima kept his word, afterwards bravely fighting for him. Here is another bank-bill, having a picture of a famous archer, whose bow the efforts of four men could not bend. The

old Japanese archers were pretty good at their work, doubtless; but
I like a gun, Ralph. What does a bow amount to before a gun?'

"Bow before gun? Why, it amounts to bow-gun, doctor.'

At the doctor's request Ralph repeated these lines, inscribed on a
fan, written by Pan Tsieh Yu, a lady of the Court, presented to the
Emperor Cheng-ti, of the Han Dynasty (Chinese) B. C. 18. They have
been translated by Dr. Martin:

> Of fresh new silk, all snowy-white,
> And round as harvest moon,
> A pledge of purity and love,
> A small but welcome boon.
>
> While summer lasts, borne in the hand
> Or folded on the breast,
> 'Twill gently soothe thy burning brow,
> And charm thee to thy 'rest.
>
> But ah! when autumn frosts descend,
> And autumn winds blow cold,
> No longer sought, no longer loved,
> 'Twill lie in dust and mold.
>
> This silken fan, then, deign accept,
> Sad emblem of my lot —
> Caressed and cherished for an hour,
> Then speedily forgot.

CHAPTER XIII.

ABOUT JAPANESE RULERS.

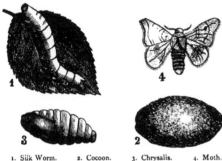

1. Silk Worm.　2. Cocoon.　3. Chrysalis.　4. Moth.

A GOOD FRIEND TO JAPAN.

FOR one day, at least, the subject of fans was the great and pressing one before the minds of Rogers Bros. The next twenty-four hours there was something else to engross the boys' attention. They soon found out that the children were a very important element in Japan life. Rick and Ralph came hurrying to Uncle Nat, their cheeks flusned with excitement.

"Oh, Uncle Nat, what do you suppose we saw?"

"I don't know; but something funny, Rick, I don't doubt."

"Yes; a lot of boys and girls round a man, who seemed to be telling a story, for he kept talking away, and they were listening and laughing. And what do you suppose he did?"

"I couldn't guess, I'm sure; but I'd just say that he stood on his head."

"He—he—went round getting money; and I rather think he stopped in the middle of his story on purpose, and wouldn't tell the rest unless they paid him."

"Rick is probably right in his guess," said Dr. Walton, "for that is a way a story-teller may have. They will work up the children to a hot stage of interest, and then will not cool them off until the cash comes in. The Japanese like to tell stories, and the children like to hear them. The better class of story-tellers have places where they narrate their stories, and charge an admission fee. I remember once I was travelling in the country, and as I passed by an open door I heard voices. As I looked in I saw a man, who, I think, was a father

sitting on the floor, and two children were in his lap. He held a bowl in his hand, and while one of the children was pouring something into it, he seemed to be telling them a story; laughing away as he went on. There are some funny stories, the Japanese story-tellers recite."

"Doctor," asked Uncle Nat, "does not Japanese history go back a long way? You tell us, and we three boys will listen."

"The Japanese themselves claim a credible history for twenty-five hundred years, but we outsiders get into the fog a few centuries after Christ, when we are trying to deal with Japan's history. The Japanese can count up a list of over one hundred and twenty rulers, called mikados. Some of these have been very famous, and eight rulers, by the way, were women. There was an empress, Jingu Kogo, who became famous, though she was not formally declared the sovereign of Japan. Japanese mothers have shown some brave qualities.

"Yes," said Rick, "I met some this morning, and they looked real pleasant."

"Jingu Kogo, I imagine, could look fierce as well as pleasant. She conquered Corea. An order she gave her soldiers is worth remembering by young people who have obstacles in life to meet: 'Neither despise a few enemies, nor fear many.'" It was her son, Ojin Tenno, who did an excellent thing when he sent to China to find out about silk; obtaining, also, some one from Corea to teach his people concerning silk. The silk-worm has been a good friend to Japan. He also introduced Chinese characters, and a better breed of horses. If I gave the long string of queer Japanese names, you could not remember about the rulers; but I want to speak of one way Ojin had for finding out a wrong-doer. He was told by the brother of his prime minister that the latter was plotting against the government, and the emperor made the informant and the minister both run their arms down into boiling water, to see who was guilty. It is said that the brother could not stand it, and was therefore judged to be guilty, and was executed."

"When was it the Roman Catholics came to Japan?" asked Uncle Nat.

"In the sixteenth century the Romanists came to Japan, and for a while they prospered; but Catholicism was almost entirely trampled out under the bloody foot of the persecutor. It should be said, though, that the

A GROUP OF JAPANESE MOTHERS AND CHILDREN.

Japanese had had some reason to complain, as all the methods for diffusing Christianity can not be approved. The Japanese showed that they could torment as successfully as Western persecutors. Nobly, though, did Christian converts prove their sincerity. Some were burned to death. Thousands were thrown down from the rock of Pappenberg, in Nagasaki harbor. Cheerfully did they let their persecutors hurl them into pits, there to be buried alive. The government for many, many years prohibited Christianity. All over Japan was set up the kosatsu, or edict-board, forbidding the religion of Christ. I have seen a famous one near Nihon Bashi. It plainly said: 'The evil sect called Christian is strictly prohibited.' That day, though, has passed away. You will ask how it is that the hated foreigners have been allowed to come again in such numbers, bringing their hated religion.

"The Dutch for a long time previous to this century had certain privileges of trade allowed them. In 1853, our Commodore Perry came here with several bull-dogs or war-ships, treating amicably with Japan, and yet the Japanese saw that the bull-dogs could growl, if necessary. Japan now agreed to open some of its ports to foreign trade. Foreign nations pressed closer upon Japan, Americans, English, Russians, French and Dutch treating with Sunrise Land. In 1868 came a civil war in Japan. For six hundred years a set of military rulers called shoguns were in existence. They lived at Yedo, as Tokiyo was formerly called, and though inferior to the emperor, yet they had such a military power in Japan that the mikado must oftentimes have been a kind of big, invisible, shut-up nobody at Kiyoto, the other capital and Japan's sacred city. The shogun or tycoon, as he has been called, had been signing foreign treaties, and not the mikado; and dissatisfaction followed such abuse of privilege. People cried: 'Honor the mikado, and expel the barbarian!' At last, war broke out between mikado and shogun. The result was that the mikado came to the top of the heap, his rightful place; and to Yedo, whose name became Tokiyo as a part of the change, he went, as Japan's lawful ruler. But now, what did the mikado party do but espouse the cause of the ' barbarian; ' and lo, the new Japan! There were men wise enough to see what was best, and seeing, obeyed their convictions. Foreign ideas are making Japan over; and among these ideas is the blessed religion of our Saviour."

"Rick," whispered Ralph.

The youngest of the "three boys" had gone to sleep over the history of Japan, and Ralph gently punched him. Rick rubbed his eyes, then opened them.

"Rick, the doctor knows a lot about Japan. Let's get him to tell a Japanese story," whispered Ralph.

A story! Rick was wide-awake at once.

"Doctor, can't you tell us a story like what the Japanese story-tellers tell?"

"Ha, ha, Ralph! Do you want me to mount a chair, and begin in style?"

"Oh, yes."

"And pass a hat?"

The boys who had spent all the money allowed for that day, looked aghast. A thought helped Ralph out of his corner.

"Pass it for the benefit of two penniless boys from Concord! Oh yes, doctor."

"We will compromise, Ralph, and not pass any. A story! What shall it be? Whew! my!"—The doctor had here pulled out ·his watch.—"Boys, my time is up, I am sorry to say. I will tell you a story to-morrow, for an engagement takes me off now."

THE LAST OF THE TYCOONS

CHAPTER XIV.

JAPANESE TEMPLE — AND A STORY.

THE doctor took Uncle Nat and his nephews off into the country for a pleasure-trip, the next day.

The boys had passed a number of gateways, around which were clustered arching trees, and they noticed that these gateways were approaches to certain buildings beyond, whatever their character might be. They were entirely willing to have the jinrikishas halt at such a gateway, that a live boy's curiosity might be gratified. Alighting from the jinrikishas, the boys shook the sleepy feeling out of their legs, and then looked eagerly about them. They saw two columns of stone, thirty feet high, and from one to the other went cross-beams. In the centre of these was a tablet, bearing an inscription. Before the gateway was a structure like an arched bridge, and two Japanese stood upon it talking busily, their heads bare to the sun's rays that fell in clear, shining light. There was a grove of trees beyond the gateway, and through the foliage the outlines of a temple could be obscurely traced.

"There," said the doctor, "the Japanese like to notice and beautify prominent places in nature by a Torii or Sacred Gate. It is touching to see the religious spirit of the people mixed up with a good deal that is irreverent, superstitious and idolatrous. They are not a rich people; and yet they have lavished many gifts on their temples.

" See those poles running through the trees before the gateway! On festival days, you will see flags and mottoes flapping from those poles, and wreaths, also. The little houses you notice are occupied by priests. When the priest is wanted, he comes out, hears the business of his caller, and, careful to receive his fee, gives the help that may be needed. If his prayers are wanted, and if it be a Buddhist temple, he may turn to a prayer-wheel, and set that to revolving.

" It is well to notice the accompaniments of a temple. Near it is a vat, where, with holy water, worshippers may purify themselves. You can find, also, in the neighborhood, a cup of tea or saké; and conveniences for lighting your pipe, if you are a smoker. On great days you would think you had come to a show."

When they had taken dinner, on their return from this trip, the boys reminded the doctor about the promised story, and he began immediately :

" Well, once upon a time there was a man, and the man had a wife. The man was very absent-minded, and so forgot himself at times as to cut up very queer capers. His wife wanted him to go to a certain temple, and beg a favor of the god; and like a good, obedient husband, he promised to go. Of course he must take an offering to the god. Gods can't be expected to do things for nothing, especially when they are made of wood, paper and paint. I think you would have to do considerable for such a god, to get anything in return. The woman was thinking what to send. Under the floor of her house was a jar, and in the jar was a rush-bag, and in the rush-bag was some coin. She took out a hundred cash and set it aside with a lunch-box for her husband. In the morning, what did the absent-minded booby do but leave the lunch-box and take, instead, what they call a pillow: a set

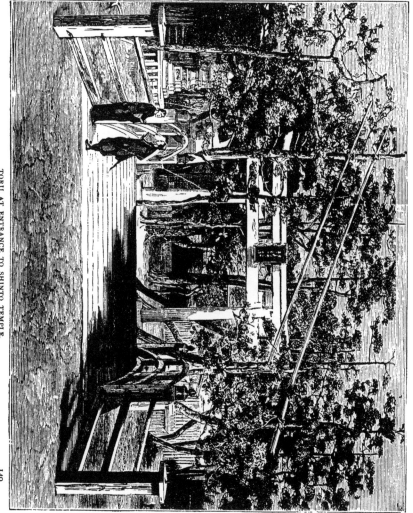

TORII AT ENTRANCE TO SHINTO TEMPLE.

of drawers containing things for a woman's toilet — her hair-pins, and so on. Off he started !

"On his way to the temple, thinking the matter over, he concluded it would not be necessary to get from the god a blessing worth a hundred cash, but a ten-cash blessing would do, and the ninety cash he could have for a bottle of liquor and a jolly time after his temple visit ! So he made two piles of the money — a ten-cash pile and a ninety-cash pile — intending to give the god the smaller heap. But, absent-minded as usual, he threw into the treasury of the god the ninety-cash heap ! He felt like gnashing his teeth, when he found out his mistake. There was no help for it, though, as the god never rectified any such mistake as that, but grabbed all he could get. There was one consolation, though, for the man, as he thought. There was the lunch that his dear, dutiful spouse had fixed for him, and he could enjoy that; but to his amazement when he opened the package, he saw hair-pins, hair oil and the like ; but there was nothing he could eat ! However, there was the ten-cash pile, and was he not a lucky man to keep a little money for himself ? He resolved to go to a cake-shop and buy something to eat.

"He saw there a large, round object, which, in his absent-minded-ness, he thought would make him a lunch ; and he bought it for five cash. This was a fine opportunity ; and so cheap ! He thought the shop-girl must have made a mistake. Fearful that she might discover it and want to rectify it, he posted off. I dare say he hurried away to so good a distance that he could not easily re-turn to mend the matter. He finally stuck his teeth into the magnificent purchase, or at least endeavored to do so, but found it was plaster of Paris — something made merely for show and to attract custom, probably ! He felt mad enough. It was dark when he reached his house, as he supposed, and he was hungry and sore and tart. He was absent-minded, as usual, and it was not his house really, and it was not his wife, also, that he saw lighting a lantern. But he thought it was his wife; and, mad and hungry, he went up to her and soundly cuffed his supposed spouse on the ear! He must have satisfaction out of something, you know. She screamed, and out came the true hus-

band, and away went our booby, about running his legs off to get away! When he reached his own home, he forgot himself again! His wife appearing, he went up to her and begged her pardon for cuffing her ears!"

The boys thought this was capital.

"Why, I suppose the poor man was so hungry he did not know what he was about, when he acted so!" said Ralph.

"No doubt he was hungry enough, and he seemed to have tried hard to get something to eat; but he was about as successful as the three dogs in this picture which I have. There was food on a shelf, and that they well knew; but a cat and two kittens had got ahead of them, and only mocked at their frantic efforts to reach the shelf and rout the invaders," replied the doctor.

"Oh — h — h!" said Rick.

CHAPTER XV.

A DOLL MAKER.

RALPH and Rick were exceedingly interested in the child-element of life in Japan, and wished they could see a Japanese school. The doctor drew some papers out of his pocket, and from among them produced a picture:

"This represents an old-time school; and yet not so very old, as the change has come so recently Look at this picture! You see the teacher and scholars are squat upon the floor, and the teacher has laid his book on a book-rest. There are the scholars scattered about.

"You notice the heads of the boys, — the hair shaven off, excepting a tuft over the forehead and over each ear. There is a child wearing about its waist the girdle, or obi. You see the children's sandals on the floor. One boy is wearing a foot-mitten that has a separate place for the great toe, as a hand-mitten has for the thumb. There is another boy who seems to wear foot-mittens. Among those scholars some confusion has been introduced.

A forward scholar is pulling by the tail a four-legged visitor. — In Japan, a cat with a tail is considered a curiosity. — This amusement provokes a good deal of attention and also attracts the master's stout ruler. In an old-time school they would learn the Japanese signs, and after a while would, with a brush and Chinese ink, make words, finally trying their hand at sentences. Some idea of drawing was acquired. The boys were taught to write Chinese characters, and knew something of the Chinese classics. Among other things, girls were required to be able to say a verse from each one of a hundred poets. Nowadays, the children are perched on benches before desks, and you will see them using slate and pencil, and you may find some American school-books on geography and other branches. The teacher chalks away at a blackboard; maps hang on the walls, and modern ideas are fast establishing themselves. It was told me that there are between five and six millions in Japan of a school-age; and that one-half of these, probably, are in school. Among the teachers there are many ladies at work. At one time, I know, they numbered eight hundred, and probably there are more now."

"That will fix woman's position in Japan," said Uncle Nat. "She has been an inferior being here, kept under by the masculine will; but where the teachers of a nation are mostly women, woman will have her deserts, sooner or later."

"Woman's Rights!" whispered the doctor to the boys.

"Call it what you please," replied Uncle Nat, reddening good-naturedly over a favorite subject. "It is only the fair thing for woman that I demand; 'equal rights,' and nothing more."

"That's so," said Rick, who was a very aged champion of the fair sex. "Oh doctor, didn't I hear you say that some of the scholars wore swords to school once?"

"Yes; to wear two swords was the privilege of a class called samurai, who were both soldiers and scholars. These gentlemen were very ugly about bowing to foreign ideas, but they came under at last. There are many in the police force, and they make good officers."

"Oh Uncle Nat," said Ralph, "Rick and I have seen such heaps of children in the streets; and there are people who get their living by pleasing the —"

"Yes, Uncle Nat," eagerly interrupted Rick, leaving Uncle Nat to guess the conclusion of Ralph's remark; "we saw a man telling stories; another, who would take a sort of paste, and he'd make it up into all sorts of funny toys, and then we saw a man eat fire-balls — and, and —"

Rick was out of breath, and Ralph came to the rescue.

"And we saw, Uncle Nat, a doll maker. He was sitting squat on the ground, his head shaved a good deal, and he had that funny topknot, you know; in his hand was a doll he was making, and he did not seem to notice us one bit."

"You would be much interested, boys," said the doctor, who was present, "in the Feast of Dolls. At a daughter's birth, dolls are given her, and these the mother keeps very choice; and then at the Feast of Dolls they are brought out and

JAPANESE SPORT.

exhibited. They are nicely dressed. There are other toys made to imitate cooking apparatus or toilet articles that a lady might need. In this assortment of mementoes you will find dolls representing the emperor and court-personages. The celebration includes a feast, and there is a happy time, all rejoicing. Dolls may be kept from one generation to another. They are as diminutive as a few inches, and then they are two and a half feet high. The week before the feast there is a great trade in dolls here in Tokiyo."

"You ought to see the girls play battledoor and shuttlecock," said Rick.

"And you ought to see the boys spin tops and fly kites!" exclaimed Ralph.

"Japanese boys love kites," said the doctor. "The frame is of bamboo, and strong paper is pasted over it. Many are rectangular, some I have seen being five feet square, and indeed they are of all shapes, and are made to resemble birds sometimes, or men, or animals; and on some there are pictures. Across the top is a very thin strip of whalebone, which makes a musical hum in the wind."

"Oh yes," said Rick, "I — I — I heard the humming overhead and could not make it out, at first.'

"The boys," said the doctor, "sometimes have kite-fights. They glue pounded glass to the string below the kite-frame, and then crossing strings they will make one saw through another. The kite that falls goes to the other side as victor. The boys, too, have a good deal of fun and exercise on long stilts. I know you would enjoy, boys, the Feast of Flags; for the day brings its games and toys. You will see figures of heroes, soldiers, wrestlers, or a daimiyo's procession. In-doors they have a merry time, and out-doors they hang from a bamboo pole a large paper fish that the wind fills and buoys up. Some-times the fish is six feet long and even more, and is a sure sign that there is a boy in the house displaying it. It is the carp that is put to this use ; for this fish, good for making headway against a stream and jumping waterfalls, reminds the boys that before difficulties they must do likewise. When snow comes the boys are sure to improve it. They roll up funny images of an old character called Daruma, who was a follower of Buddha. He spent so much time squat in religious meditation that he lost the use of his legs, and couldn't go when he wanted to. You will see his image in some of the shops, and he is a character the boys like to set up. In this picture I have here there is a snow-man, and it is Daruma, probably. One of the players has been knocked over by a missile, and it seems to amuse the others."

"The Japanese young people seem to be of a pretty good sort," said Ralph.

"Well, they have human nature here in Japan same as elsewhere. It has been said that the Japanese children are more obedient to parents than American children are, but I think you will find a good quantity of self-will and human nature in young Japan."

There was silence for a few moments.

CHAPTER XVI.

A SHORT TRIP.

THE doctor finished his story, and then Uncle Nat informed the boys that he had planned for a short trip out of the city.

One interesting spot they visited was a Japanese cemetery.

"The Japanese pay much attention to the resting-places of their dead," remarked the doctor. "They are neat, and they try to make them beautiful, also. Here come some women."

These, as the doctor spoke, came forward, and taking old bouquets out of bamboo flower-holders on the pedestals of the tombs, put fresh ones in their places. The monuments in the cemetery were of various shapes. Some were simply square stone pillars, and others egg-shaped.

"Don't they sometimes burn their dead bodies?" asked Uncle Nat.

"Yes; what we term cremation is often practiced, and is the most common way of disposing of the dead. Afterwards, their ashes are collected, deposited in an urn, and this is placed in the cemetery, and a stone erected above," replied the doctor.

"And do people have a new name given them after death?" asked Ralph; "I have read so."

158

A CEMETERY.

159

159

" Yes ; on those stones are the names now bestowed upon the dead."

Uncle Nat was silent, but thought of the passage in Revelation, where it says : " To him that overcometh, will I give to eat of the hidden manna, and will give him a white stone, and in the stone a new name written, which no man knoweth, saving he that receiveth it."

As the party pushed on still farther, their attention was often called to some novel feature. People were pursuing their trades, working in their gardens or shops.

" And that is the sign of a barber," said Uncle Nat to his nephews, pointing in the direction of a certain shop.

" See," exclaimed Ralph, " the barber shaves the head of his customer, and it is a little boy."

The boys, according to the old Japanese custom, must have their heads wholly shaved for three years after birth. Then, three tufts of hair are permitted to grow ; one at the back of the neck, or on the top of the back of the head, and one above each ear. At ten, they only shave the crown, and the boy wears a forelock. At fifteen, a boy is supposed to take on the burdens of manhood, and he may let his hair grow like a man's. That is the old Japanese style; but nowadays boys, especially in the larger cities, are beginning to wear their hair in European style, and some of the men also.

The noon of that very day, Uncle Nat said to his nephews, " Do you want to start for Australia to-morrow ? You see we must be going soon, for my ship will be waiting for me at Kobe."

Both the boys' faces began to fall ; but " ship " is an object that will revive a lively lad's drooping spirits, and this was the object reconciling Rogers brothers to a journey away from Sunrise Land.

" You see we take the big national road, the Tokaido, leading off into the country, and connecting Tokiyo with the ancient capital,

Kiyoto. Thence we journey to Osaka. We finally reach Kobe, and there we take the finest ship out, the *Antelope*. And now I have special news. Guess — guess, if you can, who is going with us to Australia!"

The boys made all sorts of wild, reckless guesses, but Uncle Nat said:

" You are wrong every time; for it is Dr. Walton!"

" Dr. Walton!" they screamed.

" Yes; for some time he has been thinking of a return to America, and has concluded to go by way of Australia, a country he was never in. So he travels per *Antelope*."

" Good, good, good!" shouted Rick.

" Better, better, better!" shouted Ralph; and Uncle Nat not to be outdone, said " Best, best, best!"

The boys thought the event ought to be *celebrated*.

" And how can we celebrate?" asked Rick.

" Let's get the doctor to tell a story, for that's the best celebration," suggested Ralph; and they hunted up the doctor at once.

" Ha, boys, you have me there," said the doctor. " Well, I'll give you a short story, one about a Japanese judge that the people think highly of, and a book has been written about him:

" There was once a young mother who had a little daughter. The mother was very straightened in her means, and was obliged to go away from home to work; and in the meantime she left her child in the care of another woman. By and by the mother was able to return home, and she did so joyfully, expecting to have her child back again, and be hers all the time. But what did the other woman do but refuse to relinquish her, claiming her as her own child! The true mother was heart-stricken, and took her case to Judge Oka; but what could he do about it? Nobody had a word to say, excepting these two women, and their testimony butted against one another like the heads

A LONELY MEAL FOR THE JAPANESE MOTHER.   163

of two enraged animals. At last the judge thought of this plan:

" 'Each of you take hold of that girl,' I imagine him saying. 'Now pull! Who is the stronger of you two shall have her! Pull! Pull! I say!'

" Both women seized the girl, but the true mother handled her child gently, and when the latter cried out, on account of the pulling, the true mother ceased, not being willing to hurt her child. The other woman had been straining like an anaconda on an ox. The friends of the mother thought she had better pull again, and the lying contestant defied her to do it; but the mother's heart said, 'I can't pull and hurt my child.' Judge Oka saw at once that this was the real mother, and gave the girl to her. The other contestant went home, probably looking sour as a pickle, but the spectators were full of praise for the judge."

" I am glad," said Rick sympathizingly, "that the woman got her daughter, or there would have been many a lonely meal for the poor Japanese mother."

" The story," said Ralph, " makes you think of what Solomon did with the two mothers claiming the same baby."

" So it does. Stories, like folks, may travel from one country to another. And in their travels, their dress may be changed like that of the new people they happen among."

" Oh another story!" cried Rick.

" Yes, yes! Do, please!" added Ralph.

"Doctor, you are in for it."

" I am afraid I am, Cap'n. Well, let me think! Hum! Let me think!"

He sat with bowed head a minute; then raised it.

" I have something now. Do you remember about our American story of Rip Van Winkle?"

" That mossy old character ? " asked Ralph.

" Yes·; and they have a man as old and mossy in Japanese stories. What makes it more interesting is that the story first came over from China, but is kept up by Japanese story-tellers; so that China and Japan both have a Rip Van Winkle. This one's name in the story is Lu Wen. He was a wood-cutter, and back of his house was a big mountain, on whose shaggy sides were the woods where Lu Wen used to swing his axe; and many a pile he hacked out for the big, roaring fires on the cold winter days. One day, in a time of beautiful weather, he had gone into the woods carrying his beloved axe. He thought he knew the paths very well, but this time he lost his way completely. The flowers, though, were beautiful and the day lovely, and as his poverty did not allow him to indulge in many romantic walks, probably he rather enjoyed this excursion and wandered on. Hark ! What was it he heard ? Something was going through the woods and step-ping on the twigs of the bushes. He looked again. There was a fox. You will find out that the fox is a witchy kind of being in Japanese opinion, and Lu Wen might have guessed that harm was ahead. If he had only been one of the famous old-time archers and shot the fox dead, how lucky ! The fox ran, Lu Wen following, and at last they came to an open place where Lu Wen wit-nessed a sight that made him forget the fox and also lose his senses ; for there were two very beautiful ladies squat on the ground, playing checkers. How handsome they were ! Lu Wen stared, and stared, and stared, the ladies not seeming to notice him at all — the rogues ! ' What a nice game that is, and I wonder who will beat ? ' he must have said to himself. He kept watching the play and the players also ; but he finally remembered that it would not do for him to stay longer — especially, you know, as neither of the beautiful witches

ONE OF THE OLD-TIME ARCHERS.

167

had asked him to sit down and have a game with her. As he
tried, however, to go away, what was the matter with his legs and
with his hands? He felt stiff all over. The handle of his axe
suddenly began to rot and crumble. He bent to pick up the pieces,
when, to his surprise, he saw dangling from his once shaven chin,
and hanging upon his bosom, a long hoary beard, white as the
snow on the mountain in winter! What had happened? He dared
not think, I imagine, but concluded that he would go home—a safe
place to retreat to in trouble. So with his stiffened limbs he went
hobbling along, hobbling along, and came down the mountain to
the neighborhood that had been his home. There were the houses,
but a new set of people was in them, and everybody was greatly
exercised over this strange old white-bearded, hobbling man. The
dogs barked at him and the children poked fun at Lu Wen. Lu
Wen's heart sank within him. Did no one know him? He asked
about his family, and then the neighborhood concluded he must
surely be a fool, as no one knew anything of such a strange family.
By and by up tottered a venerable lady who testified that away
back in the history of her family there was a man by the name
of Lu Wen, but that was six generations before her day. I
seem to hear her say, 'He was my great, great, great, great, grand-
father!' It must have frightened him to hear the old lady, for he
turned away, — went back to the mountains, — and was never heard
of again."

CHAPTER XVII.

A JINRIKISHA JOURNEY.

JAPANESE WOMAN AND CHILD.

IT was a fine spring morning in Japan, and four jinrikishas were all moving along the great public road running from Tokiyo, the new capital of Japan, to the old capital, Kiyoto. There was a jinrikisha for each traveller ; one for Uncle Nat, a second for Dr. Walton, a third for Ralph, and a fourth for Rick. What happy boys!

On either side were tall, solemn old pines overshadowing many homes, and in the distance were the glorious heights of Fujisan, white as a marble watch-tower. The travellers were often passing people; the same strange, yellow-skinned men and women, some comfortably and others poorly dressed, and they were walking on clogs about two or three inches high. Little boys were at their play. Some of these had bare,

KINDNESS TO THE BIRDS.

shining scalps bobbing up and down and sporting those queer little top-knots that amused Ralph and Rick so much.

"Oh, see!" called out Rick to Ralph.

The latter looked and saw several white-robed men under their broad hats. In one hand they carried a little tinkling bell, and in the other a walking-stick.

"Who are those men?" called out Rick to the doctor, whose jinrikisha was quite near.

"They are pilgrims, bound for some temple; and on such walking-sticks I have seen paper prayers, and those bells jingle and summon the gods to notice their petition. It is my opinion that those gods will need quite an arousing."

They soon passed temple-grounds, and the doctor promised to tell the boys about such places. Sometimes the road ran through villages and towns, and then it stretched through the open country. Stopping at various tea-houses or restaurants, they had an opportunity for several lunches, each halt attracting a throng of ambitious sight-seers. Several women gazed curiously from their homes at the strangers. One of these female inspectors carried a child upon her back — a common fashion in Japan — and the tired mother looked as if she would be very glad when this child could walk.

"What makes the women black their teeth here in Japan, doctor?"

"I don't know, Ralph. It can't be because it makes them handsome. I only know that in some regions it is a sign of marriage. Young unmarried women may do it, but according to my way of thinking, they would never catch a husband with that bait. Married women too remove their eyebrows. Female customs, though, as well as male, feel the influence of European ideas. The empress Haruko, I know, did discourage this tooth-blacking, eyebrow-shaving custom."

"The women are kind to the birds," interrupted Rick, that defender of the female sex, desirous to say all he could for them.

"Oh yes. The Japanese are, as a people, kind to animals," replied the doctor. "Many Buddhists are in Japan, and their religion emphasizes kindness to animals."

"Buddhists believe in the transmigration of souls; that mankind after death may pass into animal kind, do they not?" asked Uncle Nat.

"Yes."

"Then I can see why one should be careful about hurting a cow, lest he injure some old ancestor."

Ralph and Rick were anxious to see the inside of a real Japanese house; one that had not been invaded by any foreign ideas.

"There is a house with an open door," suggested the doctor, after a lunch-halt. "Let us go there."

The four jinrikishas halted at the open door, and as half a dozen bare-headed children came rushing out of the house, and stared at the strangers, the latter concluded that the desire for sight-seeing was mutual. A Japanese woman met the party, and smilingly acceded to the doctor's request in Japanese for a look inside.

Before entering the doctor called the boys' attention to the way the house was built without.

"There, you see this is a pretty light affair. The frame is of wood, and while in Tokiyo and Yokohama we saw many roofs that were tiled, this one is of straw-thatch. Now we will take off our boots and shoes — that is the custom, you know — and step inside."

The floor was covered with straw-matting, and the walls were only partitions of paper, and there were paper windows with paper shutters. In the centre of the floor was a little furnace or brazier, filled with glowing charcoal, on which was a tea-kettle boiling furiously.

MAKING TEA.

175

"Here," said the doctor, "the cooking is done. Sometimes you will see a fire-place in the middle of the floor; the smoke escapes through a hole in the roof."

"Where are the chairs?" asked Ralph.

"The floor is chair."

"And haven't they any sofa?"

"The floor is sofa."

"Haven't they any beds or tables ì

"We will find out."

The doctor then went up to one of the partitions, and the Japanese woman who had followed him and comprehended his desire, courteously slipped forward and pushed back the paper wall. The boys then saw that the partitions were arranged to slide backward and forward. In the second room thus revealed, they saw a wooden block and a little cushion on top. Near it were several quilts.

"The floor with the matting is the bedstead, boys, and these quilts are the bedding. You see the furniture is very simple. Sometimes you will see a little lacquer table in a room. I have seen in houses a room with a recess and raised platform for vases, flowers, and various ornaments; and the surrounding walls are decorated with pictures. Generally in houses you see a god-shelf; perhaps in the kitchen or the family sitting-room."

"I can see after inspecting this house," remarked Uncle Nat, "why fires are so destructive in Japan, the houses being just wood and paper so often."

"I was going through a town once," remarked the doctor, "and I noticed the sounding of a fire-alarm. A man mounted a ladder and bawled to the people, and they responded and pulled down the house that was on fire. That probably was the best thing they could have done. The building was a cheap affair, and it was of more consequence to prevent the spreading of the fire than to save the house.   People in Japan do not live in palaces, by any means. Some of these must be places of positive discomfort in cold weather. Japan is not that fairy-land of pleasure and luxuries that we might imagine from the talk of some."

" No, " said Ralph ; " I meet people every day thin and bony, who look as if they envied me every mouthful of food I took."

" Japan has its share of poverty," said the doctor, " while the people as a whole seem comfortable."

In the house last visited Rick executed a piece of mischief. He wanted to see how thick might be the paper in the partitions, and he pressed against it and pressed through it !   Frightened, he left the house without an apology to its mistress.

" That won't do," he said to himself.   " I am backing out in a mean way.   Besides, I have lost my sleeve-button.   It is in the road probably, and I had better hunt it up.   No ; I will go into the house first."

He turned, and entering the house again drew its mistress up to the ruptured partition.   As he showed it, he pulled some money out of his pocket and offered it to her.   She laughed, and shook her head.

" Oh yes ; take it," persisted Rick.

She shook her head again and jabbered out a quantity of Japanese words.   Then laughing, she put her hand into the sash about her waist — the obi — and pulled out Rick's sleeve-button !   She stooped to the floor and signified thereby that she had picked it up there. Rick, as he received the button, again pressed her to take the money ; but she declined.   Then he put it into the hand of a baby on her back, and running out to his jinrikisha, was rapidly borne away.

It was in the first day's journey that the doctor said : " There is a

"WON'T YOU TAKE A CUP OF TEA WITH US?"

curiosity I want the boys to see, if agreeable to you, captain. I mean the famous Buddhist idol, three miles from Kamakura."

"We will certainly go," replied Uncle Nat.

Arriving at the designated spot, the sharp eyes of the two boys were turned in every direction, and their mouths were full of questions. The big idol, Dai Butzu, interested them exceedingly.

"This idol, boys," said the doctor, "is a big bronze-image of Buddha. You see he is squat in a gigantic lotus-blossom."

The god's eyes were shut and he appeared to be enjoying a nap, his hands resting in his ample lap.

"Oh-h-h!" said Rick.

"There he is! The man whose religion is that of Buddhism believes that the final and desirable state of the good is one of unconscious rest, and the god, you see, is in that condition. Look at his head! It is covered over with shells — the shells of snails. An old fable runs that when Buddha came up from the sea, these snails travelled at a wonderful pace, for them, and clustered upon the head of his sacred majesty, making a kind of shield against the sun. Then it is also said that the shells represent the god's wavy hair."

Rick and Ralph were on the hunt at once for adventures. They found a chance to get inside the image, and they saw a number of shelves there supporting little images. Coming out again, the boys looked over the idol once more.

"He has big ears," said Rick, "and that is a good sign; for they say that folks with big ears are generous."

The last thing that the boys desired to do was to climb up and perch on a thumb of the god.

When they started to leave, the doctor said: "You will find many temples in Japan, and some are very rich in their style of arrangements within. I remember one that I saw the past season. Its roof was very heavily tiled. Before the temple-steps stood four men, their heads reverently bowed. The sight touched me, though the men were idolaters, and made me long for the time when the light of a better day would come to them, and show them the Saviour."

When twilight came they stopped the jinrikishas at the door of a public house, or yadoya. The landlord met them when entering, and prostrated himself, bowing his shiny scalp, and with his forehead touched the floor several times. The building was quite large.

" Slide back all these paper walls about us, boys, and you would get an immense room; a plan they resort to in Japan when they want plenty of space," said the doctor.

" Supper most ready ? " asked the captain, as they passed into an inner room.

" Almost, I guess," replied the doctor. " I noticed in the kitchen that things seemed to be in the condition of a lively bake or a lively boil."

They all sat down upon the mat-covered floor, and supper was brought in and placed on little low tables.

" What have we here ? " asked Uncle Nat. " Jack Bobstay has been in Japan, and we ought to have him here to give his opinion, boys. But here comes the doctor, and he will tell us."

Blessed old Jack Bobstay ! How Ralph and Rick wished him there. The doctor, who had been out of the room, now returned, and gave his opinion about the dishes furnished for supper.

" Let's see ! Here are eggs, and here is rice, and here is tea, and here is — give it up ! It is some mysterious Japanese vegetable compound. Ah, here is some fish ! "

" I can't say I like Japanese living as well as I do the roast-beef style," said Uncle Nat ; and it was the opinion of all.

Supper over, Ralph and Rick clamored for a story,

HAVING A SOCIAL TIME.

185

"A story? Hold on a minute or two. I think it would be a good idea to have a little fire, and I will ask our landlord to let us have a brazier of coals," replied the doctor.

A little furnace of hot coals, known as the hibachi or fire-brazier, was soon surrounded by a group of listeners squat upon the floor and anxiously awaiting the doctor's story. Ralph looked about him. There were the floor-squatters in that strangely furnished room, neither chair nor lounge beneath them, the brazier before them, paper walls lighted by a Japanese lamp about them.

"This lamp," said the doctor, "has a saucer filled with rape-seed oil which feeds a

OUT FOR A WALK.

lighted wick.   People are using kerosene lamps in many places."

The boys thought it would be fun to listen to a story seated around a Japanese brazier.   The doctor began :

" It is claimed that the authentic history of Japan goes back to the seventh century before Christ.   It is not easy to give precise dates, but when we think of Rome's long existence, we must remember that.Japan is at least as ancient a country, and probably has had a longer life.   The history of Japan is full of exciting deeds, bristling with strife, a great many heroes figuring in the contests.

"Japan makes me think of England, in some things. They both are islands, and both have been jealous of foreign interference, and both have had civil wars.   Just as England had its war of the Roses, so Japan had its war of the Chrysanthemums, that flower representing a kingly line.   Then England, you know, had its Spanish Armada ; that big, burly collection of old scows coming to overthrow English power. So Japan was threatened by a Chinese Armada.   There were one hundred and seven thousand Chinese, Tartars and Coreans in thirty-five hundred junks.   It is now six centuries almost to a year that this big flock of evil birds, their wings outspread in an evil flight, came toward Japan.   The birds folded their wings off the city of Daizaifu. Now the Japanese are brave.   The children are trained to despise death, and to have a very delicate sense of honor, which is sometimes very foolish and very bloody.

" The Japanese sailed out in their lighter craft, showing their spunk and daring; but though they annoyed the enemy and did valiant deeds, they accomplished nothing substantial and decisive.   They lost many lives, as the Chinese junks carried catapults or machines for throwing stones, and they cruelly pelted the Japanese navy.   The Chinese finally swung an iron chain from one vessel to another, to intercept the attacks of the Japanese.   The Chinese also sent parties to the shore, but the Japanese routed them; and they built earth-works along the sands, to keep off the invaders.

"A Japanese officer, Michiari, was pleased to see this Chinese invasion, as he had prayed for this very thing. Writing his prayers on pieces of paper and then piously committing them to memory, he finally set the paper-prayers on fire, as that is supposed to be a quick way of getting a message to a god. The ashes he swallowed! That process must have touched the heart of a wooden god, even.

"Michiari now packed two boats with daring men, and off he went to the Chinese fleet. His pigmy craft were despised by the Chinese, for the Japanese were apparently unarmed.

"'He is coming to surrender himself,' said the Chinese concerning the Japan leader.

"But the latter had no such idea. He threw out his grappling-hooks, seized a junk, and then his band with keen swords attacked and overpowered the crew. Burning the junk, they left for the shore. The whole nation was fired by such heroism, and help came from every quarter. All over the land, too, there was a going up of prayers at the temples. The emperor wrote out a prayer and sent it by a messenger to a temple, and the story runs that when the messenger reached the shrine and presented the prayer, a bit of cloud was seen that grew into — what?

"Into one of the cyclones, so well known in that part of the world; and it burst upon the Chinese fleet How it raged — that awful storm!

"It reminds one of the terrible gale destroying the Spanish Armada off the English coast. In that Japanese cyclone, the Chinese junks were swept helplessly upon the terrible shore-rocks, and many men were drowned. The survivors reached Taka island, intending to build boats there in which they could sail to Corea; but the Japanese

STRETCHED OUT FOR THE NIGHT.

came upon them, and, overpowering them, left only three to carry home the tidings of the sad disaster on the shores of Japan.

"That was an awful catastrophe. Although it happened hundreds of years ago, it is by no means forgotten, and to-day you may hear a Japanese mother referring to that great Chinese Armada, as she tries to quiet her child with the question:

"'Do you think the Mogu (Mongols) are coming?'"

After the telling of this story, the doctor and Uncle Nat went out to make some arrangements for their journey on the morrow, and Rick thought it just the time to improve his opportunity!

He heard a noise on the other side of the paper-walls.

"It sounds like a man snoring," he said. "I wonder if I can't take a peep! Let me see; I just take hold of this thing, shove a little, and slide it — back!"

To his gratification the paper screen moved back, and allowed him a chance to thrust in his inquisitive head. He saw the snorer stretched out for the night in Japanese fashion, and near him was a paper-shaded lamp, its mild lustre falling over the room. At one side of the room, the partition was decorated with a picture of Fujisan, storks and vines.

While Rick was enjoying this view, he surprised himself and others by yelling in pain, "Ow - w - w!"

The next moment he was seen rushing back into his room, holding on to a badly nipped nose. He had thrust his sharp little nose just far enough forward to be caught between the paper partition and its neighbor, if any hand might force them together, and that hand had been furnished by Uncle Nat's coming into the room, and noticing at one end of the partition that it was not in place; he failed to look at the other end and see who was there; and Rick had the benefit of Uncle Nat's ignorance.

"Poor fellow!" said Uncle Nat; "I won't do it again."

"And I'm sure I don't want you to," blubbered Rick.

A POETESS.

CHAPTER XVIII.

OKA AND MURASAKI.

ONE more story!" was the appeal of the boys to the doctor the next morning.

"Please, one more," they cried.

"Oh have mercy, boys! You will wear the doctor out," said Uncle Nat.

"I will put my hand in the bag and pull out one more story," said the doctor good-naturedly; "and this shall be about Judge Oka. One day a case of theft came before him, and the particulars were these: There was an old man, very rich, but he kept on selling pickled vegetables — his business — for it brought

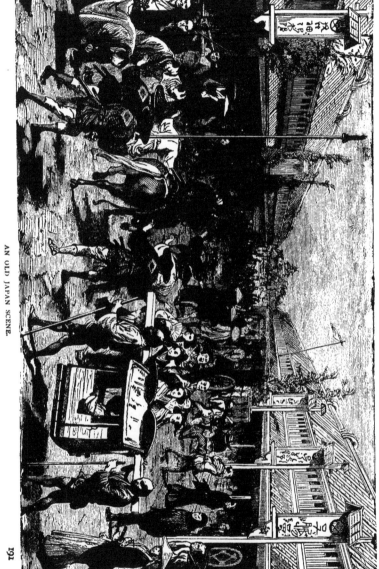

AN OLD JAPAN SCENE.

him the gold he loved so dearly. But where could he safely keep his gold, when he had it? He thought of a curious place at last. Among his pickled vegetables was a vessel of radishes. These were kept in a mixture of various things—salt, radish-juice, and so on, which, in the course of time, evolves an abominable odor, strong enough to knock a horse over, but not a miser. There, in the dark bottom of the radish-vessel, the skinflint kept his gold. It chanced, though, that a neighbor found out this precious fact. Perhaps he was looking through a window at night that had not been shut, and he saw Old Nipper — my name for him — making a wry face, as he plunged his hand down among the radishes, then showing a very happy face, as he fished up a shining piece of gold. This neighbor — alas for the old pickle-dealer! went into the shop during Nipper's absence, and putting his hand into the radish-dish left the radishes, but took the gold. What a face the old pickle-dealer made now, when he examined his beloved collection of radishes! He flew to Judge Oka and told the story. What was to be done? Did the judge scratch his head, look grave, and wonder, and then scratch again? If he did, something came of the scratching. He summoned before him Nipper's neighbors, and afterwards locked the doors. Then he went from man to man, and made them present their hands. What was the judge up to? He was up to this — a smell; for he went from man to man, and so came to a hand that carried the abominable smell of the radishes. It was the hand of the thief, and he owned up and received his deserts."

The boys thought that Judge Oka was the "smartest judge out."

"I 'spose," said Rick, "the Japanese have story-books, as well as story-tellers."

"Oh yes, the Japanese are very literary, after their fashion.

They have a great many books, and not only the men, but the women, have cultivated a literary taste. There is a book highly esteemed in Japan which was written by Murasaki Shikibu, a lady. She was asked to write some sketches, as the mother of the emperor wished for a fresh book; and Murasaki resolved to attempt the task.

"As the famous Chinese author, Shomei, when he wished to execute some literary work, put up a lofty building and then shut himself in it, she determined to imitate his example. At Ishiyama, from which one looks down upon the waters of Lake Biwa, a very high retreat was built for her. In the moonlight, the waters glistened like glass, while the mountains rose up stately and grand. Murasaki retired to the spot, and there, alone with the moonlight, the water, and the mountains, she was so fired by a literary fever that in one night she wrote two chapters of the *Genji Monogatari,* a Japanese classic; and the whole work she finished in a few weeks."

"Do not the Japanese have a great many maxims?" said Uncle Nat.

"They certainly have some ingenious sayings, and they like to trot them round. Such are these: 'Don't trust a pigeon to carry grain;' 'You can not rivet a nail in potato-custard;' 'In mending the horn, he killed the ox;' 'Live under your own hat;' 'A cur that bravely barks before its own gate;' 'You might as well scatter a fog with a fan.' A blind man walked confidently near a deep hole, and I heard another say, as he rushed up and pulled the fellow out of danger, 'A blind man does not fear a snake.'"

The boys then looked at the picture of a street-scene the doctor showed them. There were ladies, a kago and bearers, an official on horseback, and "two-sworded gentlemen," as the doctor called them. "But the day of the latter," he added, "has passed by, and this is an old Japan scene."

CHAPTER XIX.

JAPAN TEA.

I WANT," said the doctor one morning, "to show the boys something new to-day."

"All right. Anything to interest those lively youths," replied the obliging Uncle Nat.

Where the road passed through a farming region the doctor cried out:

"Let's stop here!"

The jinrikishas came to a halt, and the party alighted; the doctor led them into a field dotted with bushes that seemed to be magnets attracting several young women, and these seemed like very busy birds pecking at tempting fruit.

"Huckleberry bushes!" shouted Ralph, springing away, and followed by Rick.

"Oh pshaw!" exclaimed Ralph. "I forgot it was spring! But what are they?"

"Bring on your huckleberries, boys!" called out Uncle Nat. The doctor was roaring.

"Sold! sold!" exclaimed Uncle Nat.

The boys were of the same opinion, as their look of chagrin showed.

"Well, what do you call them?" asked Rick.

"Oh I know," said Ralph. "I remember, now, that I saw a picture of them once. They are tea-plants, doctor."

"Yes, these are tea-bushes; and, as you see, they grow to be pretty stout. They are now picking the new leaves on top—the tender growth; they gather older leaves also, but the nicest teas come from the tender tips of growth in the spring. What is sold generally in our home is the older leaf-growth, and some of it, as I remember the taste, was pretty old indeed. And do you want to see the next step in this tea-business? Come this way."

They followed one of the tea-pickers who was now carrying a basket filled with leaves, and she entered a building where several men were at work. The leaves were then steamed a little while and softened. The next stage in the process was the drying; and the boys watched it intently. The leaves, still moist, were placed in pans, and heat applied. Beginning with the hottest pans, a Japanese then worked the leaves over, and after a lengthy rubbing and rolling, the dried leaves were gathered in baskets.

"There is one other thing to be seen," said the doctor; and he led Uncle Nat and the boys to a house where the leaves were sifted and picked over. Everything of a refuse nature was thrown away, the nicer leaves put by themselves, and also the coarser growth.

"The last process I guess you all smelt at Yokohama. Do you remember any tea-odor in the street after your landing?"

"Oh yes, doctor," said Uncle Nat; "and I wanted a cup of tea at once."

"At Yokohama the tea is re-fired, as they call it; heated and worked over and prepared for a sea-voyage to distant markets; and the most of this, they tell me, is colored to suit foreign customers."

The jinrikishas were now resumed, and the journey continued.

"THE FROG BAND IS 'OUT SERENADING SOMEBODY.'"

When they stopped at a hotel that night, Rick, who had put his legs to a very frequent use during the day, dropped into a profound slumber at once; but Ralph lay awake. He saw where the soft light from the paper-lamp fell upon the paper-walls. Then he thought how queer it was to be in that room without bedstead, without table, without chair, without washstand. Hark! He raised himself on his elbow.

"Frogs!" he said. "The frog band is out, and serenading somebody! That makes me think of home."

Then his thoughts wandered far away to old Concord. He imagined himself passing into the house. He went into the sitting-room. He climbed the stairs leading to the chamber where he and Rick had many mornings contended in such obstinate pillow-fights, sure to be followed by a nap from which mother's voice would with difficulty arouse them. What heavy sleepers! So drowsy when she called; and she called now. Then he slowly crawled out to the barn-chamber — so quiet; no one there! Then he went out into the garden under an old pine, where the wind made such sleepy, sleepy music, and then he went — went — went — to the Land of Nod!

CHAPTER XX.

IN the morning the jinrikishas moved off briskly. The way led past farm-houses and fields; through villages; amid varying features of Japanese life and scenery. There were man-carts, and jinrikishas and kagos — pilgrims, policemen, farmers; but everywhere it was Japan, and everybody was Japanese. There were the same yellow-skinned, dark-eyed people, wearing their obi and clogs; not so thrifty in their looks, so well-to-do, as a New England people, and yet always civil and pleasant. Our travellers were tired, and early halted for their nightly rest. After their supper of tea, fish, and rice, Ralph came to the doctor, whispering, " I guess somebody is dead in the next house."

" Why so ? "

" I went to the door to see if any children might be there, because I thought they would like to have some of the picture papers I had."

" Some you brought from home ? "

" Yes ; that was Nurse Fennell's idea. She said she couldn't be

JAPANESE MOURNERS.

a missionary to the heathen, but she could send 'em papers; so she begged a lot with pictures, and Rick and I — when we don't forget — give them round; and, doctor, children like to look at them."

"Oh yes. They see the picture and get some good idea from it, unless Nurse Fennel sent them a bad assortment. But you didn't tell what you saw."

"Well, I saw people bowing on the floor, and they seemed to be in a great deal of trouble."

"You are right, Ralph. Some one had already told me that a death had taken place there. Did you see a screen turned upside down, and a kind of table near it; and was there any light on the table; and did you see dishes?"

"Oh yes."

"Well, behind the screen was the dead body, the head turned to the north — for the Japanese are very particular about the direction of the head. Near the body, probably, were the chop-sticks and eating-tray the deceased had used; cups and saucers also. Food too doubtless was there."

"They seemed to be in terrible trouble," said Ralph sympathetically.

The journey was delayed next day, and the boys saw a funeral procession move along the road. A platform resting on two poles that four bearers uplifted, supported the coffin. The coffin was covered with a white cloth, and the bearers wore a white dress. In the procession were priests wearing their robes; and there were the bearers of lanterns, which were of white paper.

"White seems to be the color of mourning more than black," thought Rick. Something else he noticed; and he asked the doctor about it.

"I saw the lanterns in the procession. They seem to use them for almost everything."

"Yes; that is one of the features in Japan a stranger is sure to notice. The lanterns are sometimes very large. Those used in the temples are ten or twelve feet long, and they will measure three or four feet through. They may be only a foot long and four or five inches wide; and such lanterns are carried about. They are of various shapes; sometimes like fans or fishes, then circular, or perhaps square or oblong."

When they halted that noon, the boys asked the doctor to tell them about the religions of Japan.

"There are three religions. The oldest is the Shinto. In the Shinto temples you will find special honors paid to the departed heroes, whom this religion deifies. It teaches that the mikado is a divinity. It has been policy for the government to keep up this old faith, whose special distinguishing feature is the worship of Japanese heroes.

"Buddhism is another religion observed in Japan, but it was something imported. Its founder lived in India in the sixth century before Christ, and was the son of an Indian king. His name was Siddhartha, but he was also called Gautama (a family name) and Sakyamuni (the devotee of Sakya; another family name). His title of honor was Buddha, meaning 'the sage.' There have been various Buddhas, Gautama being the last; and he declared that another would in the future appear.

"The Buddha receives divine honors, and is thought to be the supreme ruler of the present period of the world. In his images, he is generally represented as seated, his legs crossed, apparently lost in contemplation. This state of mind is thought to be a great virtue, and an excellent way of getting to the Buddhist heaven. According to Buddhism, the soul at death passes into a new form of existence, higher or lower — perhaps a superior being or a disgusting animal; according to one's merit or demerit.

"The Buddhist heaven, accessible only after many transformations, much living and dying, suffering and purifying, is called *nirvana;* a state of unconsciousness, rest, apathy, and some say it means extinction. Anyway, it must be a queer kind of know-nothing-ness. The founder of Buddhism is claimed to have three hundred millions of followers. in the world, and he has been allowed four hundred millions even. In Japan he is very popular. He himself exacted of his disciples a life of self-denial, and insisted upon good morals; but Buddhism has

BEATING THE TEMPLE DRUM.

degenerated, and as we find its followers to-day, there is imperative need of a great and radical change."

"There seem to be a good many Buddhist temples in Japan," remarked Uncle Nat.

"Yes ; and in these temples you find the worship of various Japanese deities, such as deified old heroes, so that Buddha is not the only one receiving special honor. Buddhism has been adapted to Japan."

"Doctor, why do they beat drums in the temples?" asked Rick.

THE EXCURSION OF TENGON BY WATER.

"In that way the attention of the god who is supposed to be in a state of apathy, is called to the prayers of suppliants. In some countries the idea prevails also that evil spirits may hinder one's prayers from reaching Buddha, and the drum-beating scares away the spirits. Besides these faiths, Confucianism has its followers in Japan. Confucius was a Chinese philosopher, and his teachings pertain to practical matters of duty rather than to spiritual things.

"The Japanese do not seem to object to all these differing styles of religion. They like many temples, and they fancy festival days There's a celebration at Sinagawa in honor of the god, Tengon. The priests take the shrine of the idol into the water, but the fishermen are accustomed to gather and generally obtain possession of Tengon, and away they go, giving the god an excursion by water."

"Doctor," asked Uncle Nat, "do we find God in Buddhism?"

"No, sir; not as I understand it."

"Do we find it in Shinto?"

"No, sir."

"Do we find it in Confucianism?"

"No, sir."

"That settles the case of each one of these systems then."

"The situation of the people of Japan is one to interest every man who thinks below the surface of things," said the doctor. "They have begun to accept foreign ideas, and are throwing aside their old notions. Their religion may go too, and what have we to offer in its place? A new and better influence must come into play, to move upon, steady and guide them. Then, certain Japanese qualities need overhauling. They are not as pure a people as they might be — a thing, I believe, that some of their leading men are regretting, and are trying to put away from the people. And there is not, also, that truth-telling we would like to see in a nation. But Japan will improve, and it has already begun to improve.

"Now, let the gospel of Christ come in to do its great work. The gospel was once offered, but not in a pure form. It was misunderstood, condemned and exiled. You remember I spoke of the persecution of Roman Catholics, and although the bloody work has been supposed to have been so thorough, yet I am told there were many survivors, and that at the time of the late advent of foreigners there were twenty thousand Christians still living in Japan. Their religion had been secretly kept up all these weary years. There are thought to be thirty-five hundred Protestant converts here, the Greek Church claiming eight or nine thousand adherents, and the Roman Catholic thirty thousand. There are in the Protestant missions about sixty male and thirty female workers. These figures, remember though, are for to-day. In a year — three years, five years, ten or twenty — what changes may take place, and how rapidly the work go forward !

"But that Japan may be speedily conquered, Christians have need to emphasize their differences as little here as possible, and unite heartily where they can agree. And the blessed bond of union for them all is the Cross, and the story of the Cross is the agency that will save Japan."

CHAPTER XXI.

THE CAT AND THE FOX.

A JAPANESE MISCHIEF-MAKER.

THE boys had already declared that the cats of Japan were "queer."

"And they most all," said Ralph, "have no more tail than a rabbit!"

"The cat is one of the animals that the lively imagination of the Japanese connects with many superstitious stories," said the doctor.

"Oh tell us one! Tell us one!" screamed both Ralph and Rick.

"Ha — ha! It is not safe to say 'stories' to you. Let me see if I have one handy. I will look into my story-bag."

"He has, I know," whispered Ralph to Rick.

The doctor made a great pretense of inspecting and overhauling his coat-pocket. Then shaking his head he declared that nothing was in the story-bag.

"Oh I see something," said Ralph, picking a piece of paper out of the doctor's inverted pocket.

"Ah! What is that?" asked the doctor, pretending to read from the scrap. "Osode and the cat. Hem! I guess I will tell that."

"Good!" shouted the boys.

"In a Tokiyo family, there was a female servant, Osode by name

A YANKEE KITSUNE UP TO HIS FUN.

One evening, when she was busy with her sewing, she heard her name called. Turning to learn what it might mean, only the family-cat could be seen. Of course it was not the cat calling; but then her name was again and again called, and Osode concluded it must be the cat calling. Thereupon Miss Puss. begged a favor — the loan of a handkerchief. Osode granted it, and the cat, thanking her, told her if at night, when the moon was shining, she would take a peep out into the garden, she might see something interesting.

"Osode was a woman, and of course could not refrain from taking the suggested peep. How her eyes opened! There were all the cats in the neighborhood, each robed in a handkerchief, and executing a lively dance.

"The next morning Osode dutifully told her master what was

MAD BECAUSE RECEIVING TAILS.

going on, and, as it was manifest that mischievous spirits were about, it was arranged that the next time Miss Puss wished the loan of a handkerchief, the master should rush in and look after the matter.

"But when at Miss Puss' visit, the master came flourishing a lance, she had gone! Noticing a queer-looking place in the road, he valiantly lanced it. Lo! on the lance's point he raised Miss Puss!"

"What queer cats!" exclaimed Ralph. "Would they behave better if they had tails? I guess it would make 'em *mad!*" How they all laughed! The doctor continued; "The thunder-god or thunder-drummer, called Raiden, is a kind of cat, with a human face. Over his head is an arch of drums, out of which the thunder-cat gets all the music that people wish for.

"The old Japanese idea is that it is the thunder-cat that springs on a person when the lightning strikes.

"Then there is the wind-imp, that is half cat. He has an ugly human face. Sometimes he will have a place near the temples, and the thunder-cat will be there also. The wind-imp carries on his shoulders an immense sack of confined air. He grasps the sack by the ends, and if he should relax his grip, the air will rush out and you will have wind. When he still holds on to an end, but with a relaxed grip, you may expect a vigorous blow; but if he should entirely take his hand off, then look out! Hold on to your hat, make secure all house blinds, and don't walk too near a tall, slim chimney! A violent storm will now rage and tear over the ground.

"This spirit has a bad reputation for flying into travellers' faces and scratching them with his cats' claws. Here is another animal that plays an important part in the grotesque fancies of the Japanese!"

Here the doctor, taking lead-pencil and paper, sketched a fox stealing along — dark as a shadow in the moonlight.

"Foxes are continually supposed to be playing their tricks on people; and one trick is said to be this: To induce people to fancy that a buckwheat-field in flowering time is a river, and that they will have to strip and wade through it. There is a Japanese god, Kitsune, a prankish sort of a creature, that takes the form of a fox. He deilghts in cutting up all kinds of capers; leading travellers astray and carrying off young girls.

"It is Kitsune that often brings sickness upon the children, and when a child dies the stricken mother's shadow on the wall is thought to have the fox shape. Fox-stories are very popular.

"A young man on a stormy day met a beautiful lady out in the

KITSUNE LEADING ASTRAY AN INNOCENT YOUNG CREATURE.

rain. He gallantly offered her his' umbrella, but he noticed that she did not wear a rainy-day suit, but an elegant party dress; and the rain had not dampened it in the least. He suspected something evil, and drawing his sword and strengthening himself by a prayer, he aimed a fierce blow at her. Then he took to his heels and ran home, returning, though, with others, to find a handsome fox that he had severely wounded! Fearing consequences, he went and made some temple-offerings.

"There is a funny fox-story of a man who boasted that he could fool a fox; and when he saw one he addressed it as his sister, and told it to come along. The fox followed, assuming the form of the man's sister. He invited it to a restaurant, where they had a splendid lunch. The man excused himself awhile, and sent his servants into the room, who found no woman, but an immense fox rapaciously devouring the good things there! A rush was made for the animal, but it made off. The man came back and boasted of the joke he had played on the fox, supposing it had been captured or killed. Instead of either result, the fox was gone and a big bill left behind for the man to pay.

"On the night preceding the day Kitsune is to be worshipped, the foxes are said to have their Sabbath gathering around a scraggy old tree, in the midst of an ugly marsh, and strange lights flash and flare about them."

THE SABBATH OF THE FOXES.

CHAPTER XXII.

THE BAMBOO, RAIN-COATS AND BLIND MEN.

 UNCLE NAT had made occasional digressions from the Tokaido, and, reaching a picturesque neighborhood, now turned off again, hoping to find some object of interest. The road that he took wound between hills bordered by rice-fields. There was one valley they found that had an enclosure of the beautiful bamboo, and at the head of the valley rose hills shaggy with forests of pine and fir.

"The bamboo is a very useful tree here in Japan," said the doctor; "very useful indeed."

"And a pretty tree, too," replied Uncle Nat. "It looks so feathery waving in the wind. In the East I don't know what they would do without the bamboo. When it is just beginning to shoot, you can eat it like asparagus. The grains are eatable, and, mixing these with honey, the Hindoos regard the compound as a delicacy when roasted. Then how many uses the bamboo-stem, so straight and jointed, can be put to !

"Bamboo-joints can be used for bottles, and in Borneo, among the Dayak's, serve as cooking vessels. Then the tree is extensively used for building; for masts of vessels, also. Baskets are plaited

RAIN-COAT.

from thin bamboo strips, and there is a paper made from this source in China."

"And Uncle Nat has a bamboo handle to his umbrella."

The jinrikishas halted for a few moments.

"Look at that house," said the doctor. "The outside wall is of bamboo wattles on a wooden frame, filled in with mud. Bamboo is a good servant."

"Who—who is that?" asked Ralph. "A straw-man coming?"

There was reason for this question. A peasant was passing them who wore a rain-coat. The straw wisps had been ingeniously arranged into a garment that fell over his shoulders, and hung down about his person. A bamboo-hat was on his head, and he carried a bamboo-pole over his shoulder. Coarse, thick socks were on his feet, and bound to these were rough, heavy clogs of wood.

"He goes on little crickets, doesn't he, Ralph?" whispered Rick.

EASTERN STRAW GOODS.

"Yes, and it must be handy; for he can take off his crickets when he is tired, and sit down on them."

"Straw goods are very popular with some people," observed the doctor, "and they manufacture straw shoes for men and for horses also. Then there are these straw rain-coats, like the one that man wears, and there are straw rain-mats. In Niigata they make a great many clogs, and one street is almost entirely devoted to their sale."

JAPANESE BIRDS.

On their way back to the Tokaido, Uncle Nat called the attention of the boys to some birds over in the fields:

"See, boys, those storks! and there is a heron."

"Those are the birds we see painted so much," said Ralph.

"Yes; on Japanese ware you will see those birds frequently introduced. They are much admired for the grace of their flight in the air," said the doctor.

"Japanese birds, I notice, don't sing much, doctor."

"I know it, captain. I can hardly tell why, but they don't seem to have been made with a piano in the throat."

"Here comes something that will interest you, boys," called out Uncle Nat, when they had regained the Tokaido. "There is a whole string of 'em coming." It was indeed a "string of 'em." Eleven bare-headed blind men with long sticks were poling their way over the road. Some of them stooped very much. One man seemed to be improving his opportunity and had thrust his hand into a little bag that his neighbor carried. At the same time he had turned his head away and was making a queer face at the sky, as if saying, "What a ninny is this blind man next me! He doesn't know what is going on." All their heads were shaved, their legs and arms were bare, and as they poled their way along they cracked their jokes and laughed, occasionally whistling in chorus.

"What do blind people in Japan do for a living?" asked Rick.

"Well, one thing is to shampoo people," said the doctor. "When one is tired, his joints sore, a blind man may come up, whistling through a reed, and that means that he offers his services as a shampooer. By rubbing, he takes the weariness and soreness out of the body. Some of the blind are musicians. There are blind men who are money-lenders. It might seem a wonder to you where they could get money; but they pick it up, and lending it, get a big interest. When a blind man is anywhere near you will be likely to hear a shrill whistle from him, if a shampooer."

The blind men had heard the jinrikishas, and were now scattering like a flock of sheep at the coming of a big dog. They were speedily left behind.

Ralph thought of a visit he made the winter previous to the Institution for the Blind at South Boston, Mass. There he saw the sightless pupils bending over their books, with their finger-tips feeling their way along the curiously raised letters into a larger knowledge, — "a bigger place to think and live in," as he said. He saw the work-shops where the blind were trained to an acquaintance with various useful occupations. He recalled one lady who, guided by her finger-tips, read for him several verses out of the blind folks' Bible. Remembering these things, Ralph could but hope that everywhere the blind might receive an education, and above all the Gospel.

CHAPTER XXIII

THE RAIN.

A HANDSOME OBJECT.

I AM afraid it was a bad omen, seeing that fellow in the rain-coat. The rain must be coming, for the clouds look dark and watery enough," called out Uncle Nat.

Word was passed to the jinrikisha-bearers to hurry up; and away they went rapidly.

"Hold on!" shouted Uncle Nat. "Put on your night-caps!"

Ralph and Rick knew what that meant.

The runners stopped, and chattering away, raised a hood of oiled paper that went with each jinrikisha, securely covering their passengers. A chilly spring rain was now slanting down in heavy, sweeping lines. Ralph and Rick for awhile enjoyed a ride under their "night-caps," but as they were obliged to alight several times, either for lunching or consultation about the way, the chilling rain was disagreeably felt by them. When they stopped for the night,

Ralph said, "Rick, if we could only get to a good warm stove-fire, and not one of those little brazier things, wouldn't it be nice? If we have a rain at home, we can warm up good. Oh Rick, do you remember Nan Smith we saw in the rain near our house, when the wind took her umbrella and turned it inside out, and Bob Gray laughed at her?"

Did Rick remember? He had not ceased to laugh about it to that day, and Ralph's words set him to giggling again.

"Oh we had the fun at home, didn't we, Ralph?"

"Yes, Rick," said the shivering Ralph. "And didn't they have nice stoves in Concord, too? Good, I tell you."

The boys were decidedly out of sorts with Japan and its little braziers.

BOB GRAY LAUGHED AT HER.

"I 'spose, Rick," said Ralph, "we must go into a paper-walled room and sit down on our legs like a Japanese, and hold out our hands over a few coals, and try to catch a little heat in them."

"Have a kotatsu, a kotatsu, boys?" inquired the doctor cheerily.

"What's that, doctor, the Japanese for cigar?" asked Ralph. "The Rogers brothers never smoke."

"I am glad they don't; but they sometimes get chilly and there's a remedy for it. Come this way, please."

"Does ko-ko-tadstool mean a cup of tea?" inquired Rick.

"Come this way, Rick. Ralph may take his in this room, but you can take yours in the next room."

"His what?"

The boys were very curious. A servant girl entered, bringing in one hand a shovel of hot coals, and in the other a wooden frame

THE LANDLORD'S DAUGHTER PERFORMING ON THE KOTO.

and quilt. She lifted up a piece of matting in the floor, and there was a bowl lined with stone. Emptying her shovel of coals into this bowl, she set the frame over it, and then laying down the quilt she left the room.

"Now, Ralph," said the doctor, "we are all ready."

"Going to bake me?"

"Not quite; only warm you up."

"Oh, it's what you told us about; cremation?"

" You'll see."

Ralph now prepared himself for this " oven," and taking a seat on the frame, wrapped the quilt about him.

" There," said the doctor, watching the gratified look on Ralph's face ; " isn't that first-class ? "

" Oh it's bamboo-nice. Get you a ko-stad-stool, Rick ! "

Rick was speedily enjoying his turn, and as they were in adjoining rooms, the paper-walls were slid back, and the boys could talk with one another from their " ovens." America was now forgotten, and also old Concord, with its glorious associations. What was it the boys heard — music ?

" Hear that, Rick ! The band is out."

" Doctor Walton said our landlord's girl was a musician, and I guess she's agoin' it, Ralph."

The landlord's daughter was indeed " agoin' it." She was playing on a Japanese instrument, the koto, her fingers thrumming the strings of waxed silk stretched above a sounding-board of hard wood.

They were soon ready for supper, which they enjoyed thoroughly.

" I wish I could get used to Japanese chop-sticks, but I can't, doctor," said Uncle Nat; " there's nothing like home-tools after all, so I have brought out knives and forks as usual, from my bag ; but it is encouraging to know that practice makes perfect. I read of a man somewhere in the East who had broken a law, and this was the penalty : to sit in a cask, fastened there, only his head and hands sticking out. His wife had come up to feed him. On her back was a fat little baby with a curious long top-knot. That wife would run a pair of chop-sticks into a little bowl of rice, and then run them into that rogue's open mouth, with a good deal of celerity."

After supper, while seated around the brazier, the soft light of the

evening lamp falling over the stork-decorated walls, the boys peti-
tioned for a story.

　"I'll tell you three, boys. The first is about a famous Japanese

CHOP-STICKS FOR ONE.

hero, Nitta Yoshisada. As he was a captain, he was asked to aid
in a rebellion against the mikado ; but he refused, and left with his
men. Then he raised all the forces he could, and lifting his banner
against the rebels, resolved to attack a coveted place, Kamakura.
The road to it passed near the ocean, and the evening before the
intended attack, Nitta made a speech to his men by the sea-shore.
Taking off his helmet, he reminded them that their master, the mikado,
had been driven away into exile, and that he had gathered forces
to chastise the rebels. He then made a prayer to the god of the
sea, asking him to look into Nitta's heart, and bid the tide flow
back and open a path for his army. Then he bowed himself. Seizing

his sword, he dedicated it as an offering to the gods, and cast it into the tumbling surf. The water swallowed up the golden-hilted sword.

"The next morning, as the story goes, the water had flowed back, and the army with Nitta at its head tramped on, reaching Kamakura, and attacked it to conquer it. The story has been a favorite one for illustration by Japanese artists and on bank-notes Nitta has had a place. The truth probably is that Nitta was favored by a very low tide and so reached Kamakura. It is a little suspicious that he did not find his sword, when the tide went down so far at the god's bidding.

"Now here's a story about a Japanese god; only a little story, to tell what the god of food did when summoned to bless the earth at the time of fitting it up. Facing the land, he breathed, and his breath became boiled rice; looking towards the sea, he breathed again, and lo! the fish came. Then he turned to the hills and breathed, and there appeared four-footed creatures, some with coarse hair, like bears, and some with fine hair, like rabbits. The god was doubtless pleased with the results of his puffing; but when some of them were presented, they were not acceptable to a fault-finder, Tskiyomi. The latter, not liking them, killed the enterprising but unlucky god of food. But this food-god when dead even, could not seem to stop his work of creating; for it was found that his head had become horses and oxen. From his forehead grew millet; silk-worms were coming from his eyebrows, sorghum from his eyes, rice from his bosom, wheat and beans from his loins. What could you do with such a manufacturing machine? And now may I tell you a temperance story?

"Sosano, famous in Japan myths, when going through a forest was met by an old man, an old woman and a young woman.

The young woman was crying sadly. Naturally, it attracted Sosano's attention. A Japanese lady richly dressed — her hair looped and bowed — in her long robe and her big obi, sporting her fan and her umbrella, gay as a gaillardia-blossom, is quite a handsome object anyway; and when a woman cries, who can stand it? Sosano could not. He learned from the old people the nature of the trouble: that the young woman had been appointed to be a sacrifice to an eight-headed serpent. Sosano at once offered his aid, if the reward of victory could be the young woman herself. All consented He filled eight big tubs with·that fiery drink, saké. On wriggled the eight-headed monster, but when he saw the eight tubs he smelt the saké and stopped Then he dipped a head into each tub and drank up every drop — the greedy creature! He became so drunk — so boozy drunk — that Sosano easily killed him. So Sosano saved a life and earned a wife. He gained something else, also. When cutting up the big snake, Sosano found it difficult to cut through the tail ; and what did he discover when he succeeded in splitting it, but a wonderful sword that had a wonderful name, muraku —— Oh, I can't pronounce it," — and the doctor stopped hopelessly in the middle of the name.

"If," said Ralph, his eyes flashing, " if they would just put rum to that use, — kill snakes with it, I think it would be a good thing."

"So do I; and this story is the first instance I ever knew where any good came from stuff like whiskey, when taken just as a drink."

"The Japanese have some very funny ideas, doctor," said Uncle Nat.

"Yes, some interesting ones, certainly."

"Oh," exclaimed Ralph, "I wish I could see that mat — the thing you spoke about to me to-day."

"Matsuri?"

"AN INTERESTING TIME."—A MATSURI.

" Yes, sir."

" That is an interesting time — a festival. A matsuri-procession I once saw was several miles long. Gay banners were displayed in the procession, musical instruments sounded, and I saw a legendary character represented. The people turned out in holiday-clothes to admire the show."

It was a bright spring day when Rogers brothers -neared Kiyoto.

As they journeyed on they heard the notes of a bell — rising, falling, then rolling away in soft, tuneful echoes.

" That reminds me," said the doctor, " that there is a big temple-bell here in Kiyoto that I want the boys to hear. Then there are shops and factories to be seen. It is a big place, and its situation is one of much beauty. The mikado once had his residence here. It is known as the sacred city, and the Japanese are proud of it."

A lot of sight-seeing awaited the travellers. Silks, fans, and fine porcelain are turned out in large quantities, and the Rogers-eyes must necessarily look into these things.

" That bell, doctor ! " said Rick the second day.

" Oh, I won't forget it."

The doctor led his companions to a temple where they saw an immense bell. It was struck by a heavy beam swung against it by a row of men.

" There, boys," said the doctor, " I could stand inside that bell, and Uncle Nat stand on top of me, and we could each afford to wear our tallest hat, I guess."

When struck, what tones issued from it, the echoes rolling far off ! They visited another temple, and Ralph noticed a peculiarity needing explanation.

" What are those spit-balls stuck all over the idols ? "

" Spit-balls ! Oh, there are prayers on those papers. People have

·chewed written prayers rolled them up into a ball, and then thrown them at the god. He is freckled all over with them; but he seems to be no worse for it, and the worshippers feel all the better, for they are sure then that the prayers have reached him."

"Don't you think, Rick," asked Ralph, "it would be a good idea to give a god an immense ear and let the balls drive at that? He would be all the surer to get the prayers."

"Oh Ralph, his ear would soon be all filled up, and he'd be deaf ·as a haddock. I guess what the doctor said was the way is the ·best: to freckle him all over."

Lake Biwa, not far from Kiyoto, was visited. It is a beautiful body of water, and an attractive spot for excursionists.

The next city seen by Uncle Nat & Co. was Osaka, and the steam ·cars carried them to it.

"We leave Old Japan for the New," said the doctor, "riding by cars."

"And the exchange seems good," declared the captain.

"We have a railroad between Tokiyo and Yokohama, and one in this neighborhood joining Kobe, Osaka, Kiyoto and Otsu; only ·seventy-six miles in all. They are extending this last railroad."

Rick sent his mother a letter telling her what he thought of ·Osaka.

" This is a big place, I tell you, mother, and I guess as many as three hundred thousand people must live here. There is a river and there are canals ·and there are lots of bridges, and the doctor, he knows a lot I tell you, he says there are heaps of wickedness here. We went down to a place and saw some children playing in the water and trying to fish. I saw a crab on the rocks that they tried to get off. My! If I ain't glad I was brought up in Concord and didn't have my head shaved! After we had seen Osaka, we came to Kobe where we are now. It is not so big as Osaka, only forty thousand people counting in Hiogo, the native quarter, ·but there are many of our folks here and so it seems quite natural. This

TRYING TO GET A CRAB OFF THE ROCKS.

237

is one place where foreigners (like me and Ralph) have a chance to trade and live. There are only seven of these places. Lots of tea and silk are brought here to be sent to the people outside, and perhaps I saw in the street to-day a chest of tea that will get to Boston and you may buy a pound out of it. There are good many vessels here; and some American, English and French men-of-war. We saw a man-of-war, and a boat was alongside of her and the sailors were holding up their oars. That is a mark of respect to some-body, and Ralph said it was to us who were near there in a boat. Funny, isn't it, to be in a sea-port and not have any wharves like Bos-ton ? They have to carry goods off to the ships. Then to carry people, they have little boats that we foreigners call sampans and they only asked ten cents to carry our party out to see a vessel ! Real cheap. Don't I wish you and Nurse Fennel could have a ride ! To-morrow, we are going on board Uncle Nat's ship,

MARK OF RESPECT.

the *Antelope.* I think I shall like it, but I know I shall miss Siah and Jack Bobstay and Joe Pigtail " (here especially to the memory of Joe Pigtail from whom parting had been so painful, Rick gave a deep sigh, deep, deep as the lowest button on his jacket). " Oh I believe I am about through, mother. Oh I want to say something more about those children I saw fishing. I hope you will let me fish when I get home, all I want to. You know I used to make believe last summer, sitting on a bank and holding a pole over Boston Harbor. If there had only been a hook and line on my stick !"

"The idea!" said his mother, when she had gone through Rick's scrawl, putting in the punctuation marks somewhat as they stand above. "If I had known that, I could not have had a moment's peace." And she tried to picture to herself how Rick must have looked suspending a stick over the fair blue waters of Boston Harbor!

UNCLE NAT'S FAVORITE JINRIKISHA.

CHAPTER XXIV.

SPREADING CANVAS FOR AUSTRALIA.

THERE'S the *Antelope*, boys," exclaimed Uncle Nat enthusiastically; and he stood up in the sampan carrying them, while its tanned, bony-armed proprietor stopped sculling and looked off with the others to enjoy the sight of that swift sea-runner.

"There she is, boys, doctor, and the old flag is up too! Doesn't that look good?" asked Uncle Nat.

"Three cheers for the *Antelope*," shouted Rick. " Hur — "

"Three cheers,' shouted Ralph, "for the flag. Hur — "

" Three cheers," shouted the doctor, "for the brave captain of the *Antelope*. Hur— "

" Three cheers for the distinguished passengers," shouted the captain. " Hur — "

" Three cheers for us all," modestly inserted Ralph ; and these were given.

The bare-headed sculler of the sampan shared in the jubilee as well as he could, and when the others lifted their hats, Uncle Nat saw him involuntarily raising his hand to his head, but forgetting the destitution of a hat, he grabbed the first thing handy, and gave his top-knot such a vigorous pull that the expression of his face changed from joy to disgust.   The extra fee that Uncle Nat considerately gave him was like the application of a very soothing plaster to the sore spot on his scalp, and he bobbed and chuckled excitedly.

" And this is the *Antelope*," said Ralph, preparing to mount the vessel's side.   But whom was Ralph looking at?   His face was directed toward the bows of the vessel.   Was some one standing there and nodding to him ?

" My, Rick, if that ain't Siah and Jack Bobstay ! " exclaimed Ralph.

Returning Ralph's gaze, and coming now toward the ship's gangway, were the two old acquaintances met on board the *City of Tokio*.

" Halloo, Siah!   That you?   And halloo, Mr. Bobstay ! " shouted Rick.

In about three seconds more, Ralph and Rick had climbed the *Antelope's* ladder and were advancing toward Siah and Jack.

" Siah, where did you come from ? "

" Oh, I's dropped down kind-er-easy."

" And how did *you* get here ? " asked Rick, addressing Jack Bobstay.

"Oh, I fetched up here and anchored all right. You ask your uncle, the captain."

Uncle Nat was jubilantly walking about the deck, exclaiming: "There, this is something like! I like to feel something solid under me;" and he stamped with his foot. "I would give more for two feet of ship's plank — just enough to stand on — than for all the Jim-Ricker-Shayses between here and Cape Cod. This is my style of carriage; my favorite jinrikisha. What did you say, Ralph? You want to know how I got your two friends here? That was a secret and surprise for you two boys I have been keeping all the way from Yokohama. I told Siah and Jack when we left them there that I expected to turn up eventually in Kobe, and my ship would be there; and if they wanted a job, that I would give them one."

"And here we are," replied Jack, "turning up all right, like a new ship with masts in, and sails bent, and jest about ready for sea."

"Oh, ain't this splendid!" said Ralph to Rick; "Siah here, Jack Bobstay, the doctor and Uncle Nat."

"We will go soon," said Uncle Nat; "I want my mail." That came from Yokohama.

"Japan has a postal service," explained the doctor, "and summer before last it was reported that over forty-seven millions of letters and other pieces of postal matter, including almost ten millions of newspapers, had been sent through the post the year before. The post office savings banks did number about three hundred, and there are more now probably."

Two days from that time, the *Antelope* that had for the past fortnight been loading under the supervision of Uncle Nat's first officer, was ready for sea; and receiving Rogers brothers and friends, she weighed anchor. Leaving behind her the men-of-war, the merchant vessels, the clumsy junks, the little sampans, the *Antelope* steadily pushed her way out of harbor. The boys watched awhile the retreating houses and lessening shipping of Kobe, the hills of green that walled in the spot and now began to dwindle, and then they turned to

ENTRANCE TO SUWO NADA.

look in the direction of the water. Uncle Nat was busy at his post, giving directions in his energetic way; but the doctor was with the boys, to answer any questions he could.

"If we had the time, Ralph and Rick, we might go from here across the Inland Sea. It is encircled by many islands of Japan, and is more like a big lake than a sea."

"How big is it?" asked Ralph.

"It is not far from two hundred and fifty miles in length, and it is from ten to thirty miles in width. There are many islands in the Inland Sea. The most of them have good soil and are well cultivated. In a voyage across the sea, my attention was specially called to one island, that must have been from five hundred to a thousand feet high; and it was terraced for crops. The Japanese are good farmers and know how to use their land to advantage. On that island they probably were cultivating rice — what they call the upland variety; and barley also. Many people live on the shores ' of the Inland Sea, and I think it has a coast seven hundred miles long. It has been called the Mediterranean of Japan."

"What is the Suwo Nada?" inquired Ralph.

"That is a part of the Inland Sea." .

"I wish we could cross this sea," said Rick.

"We are going to Australia, and must bear away in a southerly

A CELEBRATION BY THE SPIDER-FAMILY.

direction, going through the channel of Kii into the Pacific ocean."

"It must be pleasant sailing in the Inland Sea," said Ralph.

"Yes," said the captain, joining the party; "I can testify to that, and yet the Inland Sea has its trials. A mischievous little creature makes its home in this sea; some kind of mollusk, and he has a borer and will bore holes in timber a third of an inch in diameter. If any mollusk should be in these parts, the *Antelope* is in no danger. She is well sheathed."

No, neither mollusk below or storm above seemed to be menacing. Under the quiet sunny sky of Japan, there stretched out one placid surface of silver.

Ralph and Rick, tired of sight-seeing, went into the cabin of the *Antelope* and began to look about them.

" A mollusk ! " shouted Rick.

" Nonsense ! It's only a spider."

" Only ! There is a number of them up in that corner-web kicking about."

" Kicking about ! Well, it's spring, and they probably feel like celebrating; same as their brothers and sisters on land."

BOUND FOR AUSTRALIA.

CHAPTER XXV.

THE ANTELOPE.

THE boys were very enthusiastic over the *Antelope,* and as soon as Uncle Nat was at liberty, he showed them about the ship. There was much to be learned; for the boys' previous visit to the *Antelope* had been very hurried, and they had obtained little knowledge of this courier bound for parts farther south.

"The cabin seems like a house right upon the deck," said Rick.

"Certainly, Rick; and one name for it is that of the after house. It is for the captain and any passengers we have, and sometimes the officers. Now look around. You see this little house is divided into two rooms. First, one comes into the forward cabin, and in the rear, is the after cabin. There, in the after cabin, are our quarters."

"Ours, uncle?"

"Yes; and there will be passengers in the two empty state-rooms."

"How nice it is!"

It did look pretty, for Uncle Nat had ordered it to be newly painted and furnished for the voyage. A bright Brussels carpet was on the floor, and as its prevailing colors were scarlet, gold and black, it was a showy affair. On the starboard side of the cabin, was a lounge covered with scarlet rep. There were also a few chairs, and a circular table that had a white marble top. On one wall was a looking-glass, and opposite was Uncle Nat's trusty barometer. Overhead, was a sky-light, and swinging down from it was a lamp; and up in the sky-light, secure to its frame, was also a clock.

"What is the clock up there for, Uncle Nat?"

"When you are on the house, you can look down and see it."

On the house! Rick knew where he would spend his time. "Up on its ridge-pole too," he said, "if it has one."

"I should think the waves would break in the sky-light, uncle."

"So they would, Ralph, if we'd let 'em; but we have shutters with which we cover the windows, and then the water may smash upon it all it pleases. We generally have a motto up in the cabin, and I guess I will get it now. See here! Come into my clam-shell!"

Uncle Nat's "clam-shell" was a state-room just beyond the scarlet-covered lounge. It was larger than the other state-rooms, having a bigger berth, under which were drawers. A desk of black walnut was there also.

"Here is our motto, and I will take it out and hang it now."

Rick read the motto in its neat gilt frame: "God bless our ship."

"That is a good one," thought Rick.

"And now do you want to see your clam-shell?" asked Uncle Nat, opening a state-room door. Ralph and Rick sprang delightedly forward, Rick exclaiming: "Isn't it cunning?"

It contained two berths, one above the other. In one corner was a stand for a wash-bowl, and on the wall was a little looking-glass. On the floor was a strip of carpet like that in the cabin. Above the upper berth, was a little window allowing the light to come in, and allowing a passenger to look out.

"And we eat out — "

"In the forward cabin, Ralph. That is not so important as the question whether we have anything to eat."

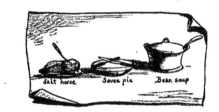

"Ah, I'll risk Uncle Nat for that."

"I don't know about that. The dining-table is in the forward cabin, and let us take a look at it. Are you hungry, boys?"

The boys confessed they were a little. They had taken an early breakfast ashore,

WHAT FOR DINNER?

and by this time were longing for dinner. Going into the forward cabin, they saw a long dining-table of black walnut, with strips about a foot apart running its entire length.

"What are those strips for, uncle?"

"Those, Ralph, are to keep the dishes in their places. When the ship is uneasy, away would go our dishes to right and left if we did not fence them in. Then overhead is that rack, and there after dinner, we can set our castors and tumblers — fitting into those holes, you see. Halloo, the cook has been in, and begun to set the dishes on for dinner. I wonder what we are going to have! Probably bean soup, salt horse, and some kind of pie."

"Salt horse, uncle?"

"You ask the cook, Rick;" and Uncle Nat here winked his eye mysteriously.

"And what is this mast?" asked Ralph, pointing to a stout mast coming down through the cabin.

"That is the mizzen mast, boys. You must learn the names of the masts. This is the mizzen mast toward the stern, and then comes the mainmast; and the one toward the bows is the foremast. And now —" Uncle Nat here went to a door in the corner of the cabin, and opening it, added: "Do you want to see our pantry? Below, you see lockers where we stow our stores, canned goods, and so on. Above, are shelves for the crockery; and you see we have to fence it in, like the dishes on the table. We hang our mugs on that row of hooks along the edges of the shelves. In that corner, you see a cupboard. Now, instead of looking at dishes, you shall have what goes in the dishes;" and Uncle Nat led them out into the cabin, where dinner was now ready.

Every hour the *Antelope* was making good progress.

"She is stretching her legs," said Uncle Nat.

"Only instead of putting her legs down into the water, she puts them up into the air, and goes that way," replied Rick.

Every hour he grew more and more fond of the ship; patting the vessel's side that afternoon, he whispered, "Dear old *Antelope!*"

Feet up ·or feet down, the *Antelope* seemed to sniff the cool sea-breezes blowing across the water, and raced still harder.

CHAPTER XXVI.

THE WIDE SEA.

"ON A HOGSHEAD, TO SEE ME OFF."

RALPH and Rick both had a touch of sea-sickness; and Ralph said he felt as if the *Antelope* were inside of him, tossing and pitching, rather than outside. But the attack soon passed away. Rick set out on an exploring expedition, and this time he proceeded to hunt up the sailors' quarters. They were in the "forward house," near the bows of the vessel, and corresponding with the cabin.

"What's here?" asked Rick, spying a door open.

He put in his head, and saw the quarters fitted up for the officers, resembling the state-rooms in the cabin, but fitted in plainer style.

"And what next?" asked the explorer.

In the rear of the officers' quarters were open doors, from which escaped a warm savory smell; and while the ever-hungry Rick was enjoying it, a dark face suddenly popped out. Popping out, it then popped in again, as if the owner had taken a sudden look at sea and sky to ascertain the weather, and then had retired to private life again. It was a funny head; both black and bald, save where two little woolly knobs of white hair projected back of the ears.

"That must be 'Old Bumble-bee,' the cook," thought Rick; and he retreated.

The cook's real name was Solomon Bumble; but the crew preferred to call him "Old Bumble-bee."

"You can launch that name easier than t'other," explained Jack Bobstay to the boys; then he said in a whisper, "It is also in accordance with the facts; for the old cook has a *stinger*, which he knows how to use."

Uncle Nat had also told the boys that the cook was "a bit testy," and he would not keep him, "but 'Old Bumble-bee' gets nice messes for the table; and then you see, boys, we have to put up with something in everybody, and with a good deal in ourselves, which I sometimes forget; but I certainly want to remember it."

The cook having once examined the sea and sky, had now put his head out again. Giving one look at Rick, he retreated into his palace a second time, shutting the door. Rick now went to find Jack Bobstay.

"And is Boson glad to be at sea again?" asked the old tar.

"Oh yes."

"I remember my going off in a ship my first voyage. My aunt was there, and she stood her younger son on a hogshead to see me off. I can see him waving his hat now. Are you goin' to make a sailor?"

"I don't know."

Judging by appearances, it would seem as if Rick intended to be a cook, so persistently did he haunt "Bumble-bee's" quarters, trying to get in.

"Jolly!" thought Rick the next day; "that door is open;" and into the mysterious sanctum he triumphantly stole. "Now I am going to see what things are like in such a place. Long and narrow; but then, it must be snug and warm, on a cold day. Two doors too; one on each side."

Rick continued to look about and talk to himself.

"Here is the stove; and what a big black one! It has got an iron railing all round the top; that's to keep the pots and kettles from sliding off. And there's a sink next the range, where 'Bumble-bee' must wash his dishes; and on the other side there seems to be a locker for dishes and so on;" and he opened the door and peeped in. "Oh, there's a seat opposite the range, where a fellow can sit down. And here's a door open. What's here?"

It was a smoky little room, on the same side of this retreat as the seat, and it contained a single berth, whose bedding testified to long and frequent occupancy. Here, Rick heard a footstep approaching.

"Which door shall I run out of? I guess I will take this one," and out he popped into "Bumble-bee's" arms! The meeting was very affectionate at first, but "Old Bumble-bee" recoiled.

Rick then saw that he was smoking — vigorously smoking — and it seemed as if the cloud of smoke rolling up from his pipe had whitened his knobs of hair.

"Ugh!" he growled; "I don't 'low nobody in dar, 'cept de cap'n orders it."

Rick humbly retreated.

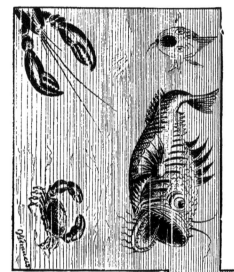

"Sides, it will be gettin' hot in here and might roast ye."

"Oh, I can stand considerable, Mr. — Mr. — Bumble-bee."

Rick, in his anxiety to "mister" the cook, had forgotten to call him by his right name.

"Who tole ye to call me dat way ?" he asked testily.

"Oh — I mean Mr. Bumble."

"Dat sounds more 'spectful."

Bumble-bee, though propitiated, did not feel inclined to let the boy stay.

"I must be gwine now, and lock up !"

"I am hungry," said Rick pitifully.

"You must wait for your supper."

"Don't you have anything left over when we have eaten dinner ?"

"I gibes it to de fishes ; dat is, de leavin's."

THE FISHES TAKING BUMBLE-BEE'S "LEAVIN'S."

That closed the last door of hope, and Rick moved out of Bumble-

bee's dingy palace, and began an investigation in the unvisited portion
of the forward house. To the explorer's delight, he found an open
door near the bows of the vessel.

"It must be the forecastle," exclaimed Rick; and he thrust in
his inquisitive head. "Who is that so chunky sitting on a chest?"
he thought.

The "chunky" sailor turned and sang out merrily,-"Ho! Boson, you
here?"

"And you here, Mr. Bobstay?"

"Of course. Come in and see Old Neptin in the forec'stle."

"This is the for-for-castle?"

"Yes; don't you see the sleeping-places?"

There were twelve berths round the dusky little hole.

"Well, where do you sit? Don't you have chairs?"

"Saltpetre! what a boson. We sit on these 'ere kids," and Jack
slapped the battered blue chest he occupied.

Rick saw three little windows, admitting a kind of twilight into
the forecastle; and a funnel-hole above showed that a stove had been
there some time.

"And this is all?" asked Rick.

"All? Yes; did you expect more?"

Rick did not answer, but inquired for Siah.

"Siah? There is his berth, but I don't know where the occupant
is."

Rick here took out of his pocket a brilliant little picture of a forest
in autumn, and pinned it to the dingy wall.

"There! Doesn't that look better?"

"Boson goin' to brighten and fix up this old hole?" Jack Bobstay
laughed at the idea. Those dirty walls, the blackened funnel-hole,
the disorderly berths, did seem so forlorn!

CHAPTER XXVII.

MAN AT THE WHEEL AND MAN IN THE MOON.

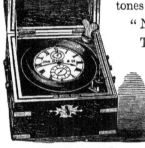

THE CHRONOMETER.

"WHO is that steering?" asked Rick one morning, catching a glimpse of a man's head aft of the cabin.

"He is the man at the wheel," said Ralph in tones of pride at his vast nautical information.

"No, it ain't. It is Jack Bobstay."

That magical name started up both of the boys, and they flew along, taking different sides of the ship, aiming, though, at the same beloved object, Jack Bobstay, and colliding with him in a style of so much emphatic affection that "the man at the wheel" was almost knocked over.

"Come, youngsters," roared Jack good-naturedly, "you are wuss than a squall of wind in the Bay of Biscay."

"Excuse us," said Ralph. "We were in a hurry to get to you."

"Good deal of the gentleman about them rough-and-tumble youngsters," thought Jack.

"What's this?" asked Rick, eying something he did not understand.

It was a case fastened to the cabin-wall, and divided into little compartments. In one was a clock; in a second, a lamp; and in a third, a compass.

" What is that ? The binnacle, we call it. It is handy, you know, when you are steerin', night as well as day."

" But I should think the sea in a gale of wind would wash into those places and break the things."

" Oh, there are little wooden slides — don't you see 'em ? We clap 'em right over the binnacle, and she's tight as a ship right after the calkin' and paintin.' Then you see that bell next you ? Right over the binnacle, I mean ; and you sometimes hear it a-goin'. I am the one when steerin' to watch the clock, and strike the — "

" Oh I know what that is," said Ralph, anxious to show that he did know some things. " And I've seen a chromo — "

" A chromo ? Them were very fashionable last time I was at home."

" I mean Uncle Nat's chromom — "

" Oh chronometer ! Yes, yes, you're right," said Jack, kindly.

" And Uncle Nat said he'd show it about this time," affirmed Ralph, rather glad to retreat, and take with him his chagrin at his mistake. A rush for Uncle Nat was now made by Rogers brothers, and they found him in the cabin bending over his chronometer.

" Oh boys, you here ? I believe," he said, raising his eyes to the clock, " I said I would show you my chronometer about this time."

" Why, it is a big watch, uncle ?" ·

" Yes, Ralph, only it keeps time much better than watches generally. Great pains are taken with it, and the intention is to have it as perfect as possible. You see it is put in a good, first-class box, and no matter how much the ship rolls, the chronometer is set so as always to stay level."

Having seen Uncle Nat's " chromo," Ralph was now anxious to see his spy-glass, and Uncle Nat very obligingly produced the ship's glass.

" Don't you remember what you told us about the sun, when we were in the steamer ?"

" Yes ; Ralph."

" Well, I would like a good chance to see the moon through a big glass."

".I hope you may have as good a one as I had once."

" How did the moon look, uncle ? "

" It looked very rough, Ralph, for there were spots all over it, and some were bright and some were dark.   It was once thought that the shady spots were water, and names were given accordingly; one was called the Sea of Tranquility, for example.   But those seas seem to have all dried up now, or gone somewhere, for astronomers have come to the conclusion that they are not seas, but great level tracts, and the bright spots are mountains, because in the sunlight they cast a shadow as a mountain would.   I have a book," said Uncle Nat rising, " that gives you a picture of the surface of the moon. (Here it is; I've found it.   See the mountains, how sharp some of their tops are, and others are round and seem to be hollow."

" Why, uncle, they look like a volcanic country in winter."

" Well, they are considered to be dead volcanoes.   There is one moon-volcano whose crater is over fifty miles across, and its sides run up eleven thousand feet.   You said ' a volcanic country in winter,' and that is what I guess the moon is ; a kind of white, wintry icicle."

" A cold place for the man in the moon," said Rick.

" But splendid when the sun lights it up," rejoined Ralph.

" How do you know, Ralph," asked Rick, " that the sun lights it up ? "

" Guess I know what I'm taught at school, sir," said Ralph proudly.

" Here, boys," asked Uncle Nat, anxious to ward off discussions about the cold moon, knowing them sometimes to be very hot, " wouldn't you like to look through a glass big enough to show you the moon like that ? "

A VOLCANIC COUNTRY IN WINTER.

259

"Where could we find it?" asked Rick.

A call for the "cap'n" came from "Bumble-bee."

"Boys, I will tell you about telescopes to-morrow," said Uncle Nat.

CHAPTER XXVIII.

ABOUT TELESCOPES.

TELESCOPE AT CAMBRIDGE, U. S.

THE next day Uncle Nat told the boys about telescopes.

"There is a very fine one at Cambridge, in Massachusetts. The object-glass, and that is the glass at the telescope-end, next to the object looked at, measures fifteen inches across. Here is a picture of it. You see that the roof over it is shaped like a dome, and a hole in the dome allows any observer to point this telescope at the heavens. Then the dome is made to turn by means of machinery, so that the telescope can be pointed at different parts of the sky. Look at the chair, too, where the man sits; for that can be moved about on rails you see encircling the telescope, and there is a contrivance for lifting or lowering the chair. There is a telescope in Washington that has an object-glass measuring twenty-six inches in diameter."

Rick thought it would be nice sometime to slip down from Concord and ride in that "cunning chair" at Cambridge, while Ralph inquired how they could " keep a telescope from wriggling."

"They are very particular about the support of the telescope," said Uncle Nat. " In observatories often, the telescope rests on a solid tower built up from the ground. That makes it very steady. If resting on the floor of a building, it would shake with the building. When a man is looking at a star, he can not bear to have the telescope jarred in the least. One of the planets is Saturn, and you do not know what a beautiful object it is when seen through a telescope of good magnifying powers.

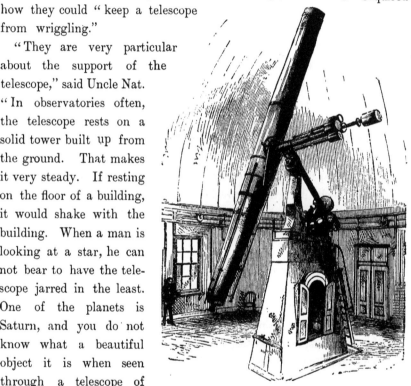

TELESCOPE AT WASHINGTON.

I will tell you about it sometime when I have a good chance."

After this talk with the boys, Uncle Nat went out to promenade the deck with them. When they had strolled as far as the forecastle, seeing Jack Bobstay in the door, mending his pants, they stopped for a little chat.   "Have you seen the latest improvement, sir!"

"No, I haven't, Jack."

Jack pointed out Rick's autumn-picture on the wall.

"You don't know how that brightens things, cap'n."

"Y - e - s," said Uncle Nat, as if occupied with other thoughts. He was saying to himself: "If my nephew is doing something here, why doesn't the uncle?"

"Jack, this for'c'stle looks dirty, and I wonder if we can't fix it up? How would an oil-cloth look on the floor — bright and pretty? Would the men like it?"

"Like it! I guess so; and I believe it would set us to improving the place all we could."

"I would paint it, but it would make a dirty job for you now. I might touch it a little overhead" — and he looked at the dirty funnel-hole —"and when in port we will paint it gay."

"Cap'n, we will have a 'For'c'stle Improvement Society,' and do our best, sir."

The crew took a great interest in the plan. The floor was scrubbed, bunks were scrubbed, walls were scrubbed; the captain sent a few pictures from a lot he had in his state-room, adding the oil-cloth for the floor, and a paint-brush, "to touch up here and there," and putting in a cushioned settee, also.

"Amazin'," soliloquized Jack Bobstay, as he faced Rick's picture, "what a little beginnin' may lead to, and especially a beginnin' by a child."

Uncle Nat was a Christian by name and at heart. He believed in treating a sailor as a man, and tried to sail his ship by the chart of the Golden Rule. Some sailors tried to take advantage of this, but, as Jack said, "he was a cap'n, while a Christian."

"The cap'n's hand is on the helm, and he has a knack at makin' a feller feel it; but he will do it in a gentlemanly way," said Jack.

Uncle Nat was particular to keep Sunday on board his ship, and he believed it had a good effect on the men. Every man off duty was expected to attend morning service in the cabin. Assisted by the doctor, Uncle Nat read certain portions of the prayer-book, the men responding and joining in the singing.

"Rick and I have joined the choir," Ralph wrote home after their first Sunday.

That first Sunday! It was a day of much beauty; and after the service, it seemed to Doctor Walton's reverent nature as if the many, many waves smiting together their restless tops, and the wind humming, whistling, roaring through the rigging, were all lifting up their voices to God in one grand chorus of praise.

WHAT THE WAVES COVER!

CHAPTER XXIX.

CORAL ISLANDS AND CORAL.

CORAL.

THE voyage before the *Antelope* was not to be a short one. Uncle Nat said, "We are going to Australia, but New Zealand is the land first to be visited."

Day after day they sailed in a south-easterly direction, passing island after island that gemmed the Pacific. Sometimes they came quite near some coast of green swelling out of the water, only to subside again, and then melt like a gem of emerald in a dissolving sea. Rick was puzzled about the equator.

"Won't we find it hot when we cross the equator, Uncle Nat?"

"Oh, perhaps not. The sun may be clouded, you know. What do you think the equator is, a kind of red hot line stretching through the water, and sizzling all the way, Rick?"

Rick could not say.

When his uncle told him one morning that they had crossed the equator, he felt quite disturbed to think he had been ignorant of it, and that the event had passed off so quietly.

"We did not melt, surely," said Uncle Nat; "and on the other hand we had quite a cool wind to keep us company."

How the wind did blow a few days after that! Siah had occasion to remember the uneasy sea that came with it. He had been assisting Bumble-bee, who was getting up a special dinner — a chowder. Rick took a fancy to it, and as he said he could not wait for dinner, being "awful hungry," Siah with the air of a grandpa, had told him: "Chile, you shall have a bowlful forehand."

He filled a bowl and started for the cabin. On the way he heard Bumble-bee's voice calling him back. Setting his bowl on a little shelf outside the forward

"SUTHIN'S COMIN" — AND SUTUIN' CAME.

house, and sniffing at its contents, he began talking to himself:

"Jes 'say to de cap'n dar's suthin' nice comin' to-day, Siah."

"Suthin' nice comin'," he repeated, and was about reaching

up his hand after the bowl. At that moment the sea gave an extra pitch, and, as he was saying again, " suthin' nice comin'," down tumbled the bowl of chowder! Siah saw it on its way, and turning round tried to dodge it, only to catch its contents on his dark locks, now covered with a savory but unwelcome cap.

"Anybody lookin'?" thought Siah.

There was a roar from three or four dark woollen shirts near the forecastle, and Siah was glad to steal away and wipe in secret the new kind of hair-oil from his head.

That day Ralph and Rick both declared to Jack Bobstay that they saw " bushes " off in the water.

" Bushes, boys! Those are coral islands."

" Oh, tell us about them."

" Well, I have been on them, and so know something about them; but if you want a full account, sure and reliable, you go to the cap'n."

Uncle Nat acceded to the boys' request for information; and that afternoon they were all upon the quarter-deck, ready to take up the interesting subject of coral and coral islands.

" May I not get Siah, uncle? "

" Yes, Rick, if he is off duty."

" And may I come too? " asked the doctor.

" Oh, certainly."

The captain was soon ringed by a circle of listeners, and no one was more attentive than Siah, who regarded Uncle Nat's head as a kind of book-case packed with volumes.

" You want to know something about these coral islands we occasionally pass. Let us then begin with the coral itself.

" To produce coral a little animal is at work, called a polyp; a tiny creature having a mouth, having also a stomach, and that is about

all there is to it. Around this mouth are long little feelers or tentacles
that play in and out, taking up and then expelling the matter. The
sea water leaves behind its calcareous or limy matter, which is deposited in very thin strips in the sack or body. The lime-matter left
behind is the coral which keeps increasing as the polyp begets children
in the form of buds; for these develop into coral-making factories,
and go to work very soon.

"The coral-buds are sometimes sprouted sidewise, and then the
coral branches out like a tree; or the polyps may take a notion to
arrange themselves so as to form a convex surface, and keep growing
that way, in which case you have a kind of dome. Coral is very
beautiful in some of its colors and shapes. Its forms have been likened
to fans and even flowers, but the gardens that these bloom in are at the
bottom of the sea. Sometimes coral is shaped like a vase covered with
a flower-like growth."

The captain paused.

"Well," said Siah, who was quite a utilitarian, "these are pretty; but
what good do dey do?"

"In various ways they are useful, and here is one: What we call
carbonic acid in the atmosphere is very essential, but it may be ex-
cessive, and so the plants, trees, gardens and forests take it up. This
carbonic acid is in the rivers in the form of lime-salts, and that too
much may not get into the sea, it is thought that the little polyp has
its mission; taking up the limy water and retaining the lime as coral.
That, though, is only an opinion."

"And then they build islands, uncle, don't they? They are useful
that way."

"Yes, many islands and reefs are built in that way. Off Australia is a
reef with occasional gaps, over one thousand miles long. Some are ring-
like, and the people of the Maldive Islands call them atolls. Matter will

collect on this coral-ring, seed and soil finally gathering there, and the next thing to be seen is a cocoa-nut tree; and then by and by a whole grove is there. Outside these atolls roll the breakers, rushing violently up the beach of powdered white coral; but within the atoll, the water is smooth and placid. The color of the inside water is that of a bright green."

"Sea-water! How can de sea-water get in? Io ie corals leab a door open in de ring?" inquired Siah.

"There is generally an entrance to these atolls, rings or lagoons, as

A LAGOON.

they also are sometimes called, the water flowing in and out; and as the entrance is on the leeward side, it is a smooth one. Whether the polyps leave that gate open, I can't say. It has been thought that they build on the tops of sunken land, hills and the like, and the opening is that natural one where the water among the hills once found its way out, and the ocean-tides now keep it open. The polyps can not work at a point deeper than twenty or thirty fathoms beneath the surface of the water, but on the eminences of this sunken land they can easily build. When the land sinks still further, it carries the coral formation down to depths below the point where the animal can work; and this explains why his work is found so far below the ocean's surface."

"How is it," inquired the sagacious Siah, "dat de openin's 'mong de hills fur de scape ob de water should always be on de leeward side?"

"You must not ask too many questions," said Uncle Nat laughing. "They will upset any theory."

In the consciousness of an increase of knowledge, Siah had a new strut all that day. He took it upon himself to attempt the enlightenment of Bumble-bee, who rewarded him by saying that he had never heard "sich a mess of nonsense in all his life. Dose polypusses de cap'n tole about, is jest childish! Coral grows kase — it do!"

Siah only wished that he had the books out of which he could confute the ignorant Bumble-bee.

"Ef I could only read," he sighed to Ralph in secret.

"Can't you read?"

Siah shook his head.

"Don't you know your letters?"

"Only as fur as pot-hooks," and there came another mournful, despairing shake.

"Pot-hooks? What letter is that, s?"

Siah nodded.

"I'll put you through, Siah, and don't you worry."

Within twenty-four hours Siah was master of the alphabet. He then prepared himself to take up a-b, ab, and a-p, ap, declaring that he felt as proud as his cousin John C. Fremont, when some "pusson at a ball stuck two posies into his hair."

Very soon Siah learned something else. He was near the boy.

and Uncle Nat one evening, when Ralph exclaimed, "Do you remember you said something about Saturn one day, when talking about telescopes, and said it was a beautiful object seen through a telescope?"

"Yes, and I promised to tell you about it. Do you want to see a picture of Saturn?"

"If you please."

Uncle Nat brought a book from his state-room and showed the famous planet to the young people.

"There," he said, "if you can, imagine a body in volume seven hundred times larger than the earth, encircled by such rings. You see that there are three; but the innermost can only be seen through a telescope of great magnifying powers. These rings are regular in form, being concentric, or, having the same centre. You can imagine how magnificent — to a Sa-turnian — must seem those vast arches sweeping above the planet. Then

SIAH'S COUSIN.

Saturn has eight satellites or moons, the largest compaing with mercury in size. Light up the arches, kindle up the moons, and the heavens to a Saturnian must be marvelously grand."

The party now left the cabin, when Rick said, "Oh, see that shooting star!"

It flashed downward like an arrow of fire, quenched at last in the sea.

"Where do they come from, uncle?"

"That is a question, Rick. Once people said they came from

the moon — out of its volcanoes; but now the theory is that millions of these fragments are journeying about the sun, and sometimes the

earth cuts across their path, and then they come showering down through the air.

In November and August — toward the mid-dle — w e s e e more of them. Sometimes they burst, and their fragments a r e scattered u p o n the earth. You will see accounts in the papers of m e t e o r s that have struck the earth and been picked up. They have been found weighing over one thousand pounds in this country, and a large one is in the Smithsonian

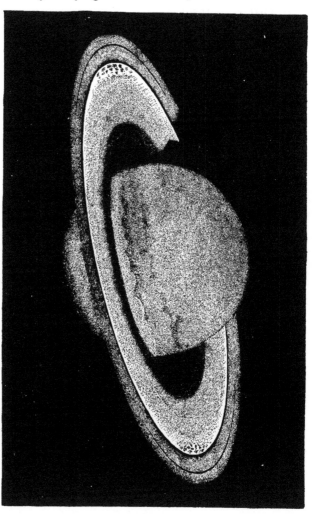

THE FAMOUS PLANET.

Institute at Washington. South America boasts of one exceeding all others in weight."

"What is in them?"

"What are they composed of? Iron, mostly, nickle coming next; phosphorus also, and other substances. They were known in ancient times. Pliny speaks of one big as a wagon."

"How big was de wagon?".

"Siah, you ask too many questions."

"What do they call shooting stars, uncle?"

"Meteors; meaning, in the air; or aerolites, air stones; or bolides, meaning things thrown — balls."

Siah told Bumble-bee all about this wonderful subject. He was disgusted, especially with the new names.

"Eber since I was a boy, dey call dem shootin' stars; a plain name, and well known in de fust circles. What was the cap'n's last name?"

"Bald — bald — bald-di-dese, I b'lieve."

And Bumble-bee was still more disgusted.

CHAPTER XXX.

NEW ZEALAND.

THEY were now sailing near the coasts of New Zealand, which rose in slopes of soft azure above the rolling waters of the Southern Pacific.

"Boys," said Uncle Nat, "I have something to propose. There are books enough in the cabin to help you. I want that you should learn all you can about Australia and New Zealand. Ralph. you may take New Zealand, and at another time Rick may tell about Australia — write up an article, boys!"

For these important papers, there was a good deal of preparation, and for several mornings the boys' heads were almost hidden behind barricades of books. There was great interest manifested in the reading of Ralph's article, which antedated Rick's production a number of weeks:

" 'The first European who visited New Zealand, was Skipper Tasman in 1642, and being a loving Dutchman, he gave the place a name after a district at home. It now belongs to England. The principal islands in New Zealand are Stewart's, South or Middle, and North. We are going to the North Island, and hope soon to anchor in Auckland harbor. In all, there are as many as a hundred thousand spare — I mean square miles in New Zealand, and it would take a line eleven hundred miles long to measure from one tip of New Zealand to the other, and one of three thousand one hundred and twenty miles, to go round the coast. It is not so very wide — the greatest width at any point being two hundred and fifty miles. Next to Concord, it must be a pleasant place to live in; for the thermometer doesn't go up so very much in summer, or so far down in winter, but stays about where one would like to have it. When we have our winter, they are having their summer. Their winter starts in June, their spring in September, their summer in December, and autumn in March.' That is a kind of turning of things upside down.

" Jack Bobstay who has been in New Zealand says there is fine land, big forests, and lots of volcanoes; and some volcanoes that still spit fire. There are springs, too, that spout hot water. There is gold, and there are lots of coal, and there must be a half a million of people, and any quantity of sheep.

" The first inhabitants are called Maoris, and they have been a pretty rough set, and are mostly in North Island. They did like to make themselves hideous in war by tattooing; but tattooing is going out of fashion. Capt. Cook did a good thing for the people by bringing here various vegetables, and among them was the potato. He let loose some pigs, also, so that the New Zealanders have plenty of pork, and as it runs wild in the forest, a man can get it for nothing, provided he can shoot it. I think Jack Bobstay is right when he says New Zealand has a future before it." ·

A good word was said for Ralph's effort, " for," said Uncle Nat, " it is in a nutshell, and you can pick out the meat quick. I think, myself, that New Zealand has a fine future before it, as you say Jack Bobstay believes."

"Yes, uncle, Jack Bobstay has been round a good deal, and has a pretty good knowledge of things."

The boys were always ready to say a good word for the honored Bobstay.

" If he had only had a chance, uncle," said Rick, " he might have made something handsome."

" Well, that is true ; but if boys would only improve the chances they do have, the world would fare better."

Jack always had a yarn ready for the boys. He told them that very day about "touching up" the *British Lion* when in an English port.

" It fell to me, boys, to paint round the bows of the ship, the figure-head, and so on. I tell you, youngsters, being a Yankee tar, I painted that lion faithfully, and I couldn't help putting a streak into that lion's eye to represent a scratch from the American eagle. I don't know as it was just the thing, but then a man must be true to his country."

CHAPTER XXXI:

AUCKLAND.

A MARINE FLOWER-POT.

"SPLENDID!" said Uncle Nat, and in the exact sense of the word, was the view splendid. A bright New Zealand sun was shining down on sea and land, as the *Antelope* moved into Auckland Harbor. A strong wind was behind it, and before it were the many little waves, each foam-crested, as if they were hammocks of blue in which white sea-gulls were sitting and swinging. On one side of the entrance was Ranjitoto Island, lifting into the air three volcanic peaks, their concial shapes suggesting three tents. On the other side was North Head, carrying two more volcanic peaks. On either side was a deserted encampment of fire-gods.

"And that is Auckland, Uncle Nat?"

"Yes, Rick, that is Auckland; and she is a beauty!"

The homes of almost thirty thousand people were massed on the rising ground before them, while at its wharves tapered the masts of vessels belonging to various nations. But Auckland is noticed in a letter from Ralph to Nurse Fennel. He commenced with a reference to Uncle Nat, and the information he gave his nephews.

"You don't know how many things Uncle Nat and Dr. Walton tell us about. Uncle Nat tells us more about the sea, and last night he showed us some queer but pretty things in a picture book. I shall have to go to the book and get the name, and here it is put down as *actinia* or *sea-anemone*. There is a kind of bag, the bottom sticking to the bed of the sea, and then they keep what they call tentacles shooting up out of the mouth like branches of a plant, and the whole Uncle Nat called a marine flower-p to And if you will believe. it, what seem to be the

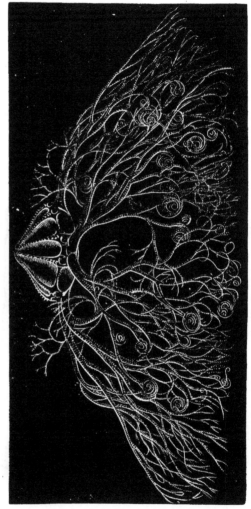

A FAN "HANDSOMER THAN ANYTHING IN JAPAN."

blossoms are the parts with which they seize their food. And Uncle Nat said if they feel like walking, they upset themselves, stand on those long branches or arms, and walk off!

"Then he showed us what he called a fan, and said it was handsomer than anything in Japan. It is really a kind of jelly-fish, and it throws out long, delicate tentacles. Uncle Nat says he has been in places where jelly-fish send out a light; he calls it phosphorescence — a hard word — and it lights up the waters in motion, and he has told breakers that way. He says the sun-fish that come ashore in Boston Harbor, after a storm, are relatives of the fan-fish.

"But there, I was going to tell you about Auckland. If you put on your

MEDUSÆ OR JELLY-FISH.

specs, you will see Auckland on the map, in the northern part of North Island, New Zealand, and it is nice to get among our own people again. This city is in a very narrow part of the island — not more than six miles wide — so that the city has two harbors, and two seas come tumbling into them. About a mile from the city is Mt. Eden. It used to spit fire all the time, auntie, but it is plugged up now, and quiet as a lamb. Uncle Nat took us in a carriage to the foot of the mountain, where we got out, and then climbed for about half i hour to the top. It was a splendid view down on Auckland, then across to the sea, and then off on the mountains. They call the hole where the fires come out of the mountain, the crater — and we went down into it. Rick felt round with his hands to see if he couldn't find a warm place, for he told me

YOUNG JACK BOBSTAY.

he thought if we did we might get a crowbar and drive it down and see the fire spout. Ain't Rick a great boy? It was easier getting down into the crater than up out of it.

"There are some nice stores here in Auckland ; railroads that go off into the country ; gas lamps, paved streets, a botanical garden and the telegraph. It is a smart, lively town, I think, and has some pretty places. The big Pacific Mail steamers call here, so that it is quite handy, if you feel like coming out. You know there is gold in New Zealand. They find it in places in the rocks, and then they say there is gold on the sandy beaches, and the gold hunters are called beach-combers, and they think the sea in storms brings the gold ashore, but they say it really comes down the rivers, and so into the sea. I don't care where it comes from, if some would only get into my pocket."

Ralph closed his letter affectionately, and then went off to find Jack Bobstay.

"I have just written a letter to my auntie, Mr. Bobstay."

"Your auntie?"

"She is not really, only our old nurse."

"It is nice to have somebody you can call auntie, and I did have one years ago."

Then Jack told Ralph about his boyhood, and the fishing village

where he lived with an aunt. He told about the bluffs back of the beach, what he did, how he dressed, his boat, and his dog Fido. He did it so graphically that Ralph seemed to see a boy in a boat grasping the oars, a dog at his feet, a coil of rope behind him, while drawn up on the shore were several fishing-boats.

"That was when I was young Bobstay," said the old tar, "and now I'm just old Jack Bobstay."

OLD JACK BOBSTAY.

CHAPTER XXXII.

THE MAORIS.

RICK.

"Who are those, uncle?" asked Rick.

Uncle Nat was riding out into the country with his nephews, accompanied by Mr. Arden, a New Zealand acquaintance.

"Those, those are —" and Uncle Nat stopped.

"Those are Maoris," said Mr. Arden, answering for Uncle Nat.

"Maoris? Oh, I remember Ralph told about them," added Rick, "in his piece on New Zealand. They are the real natives."

The men in this group of Maoris were stalwart and tall; a little darker than Spaniards. Two women were with them, dressed in dirty calico gowns and wearing ornaments of green stone. The hair of these women was curly and long, and their eyes black enough to go on a blackberry bush. One held a pipe between her teeth, and tattooes were on her face. During this visit the doctor had taken out his pencil and sketching paper, and he began to draw the face of the elder woman. But the subject of the sketch was not pleased with it, and told the doctor the reason; because he had omitted the tattooing on her face.

"Oh, is that it?" said the doctor. "I always mean to be ac-

A TRAP FOR THE SAVAGES.

commodating, and can easily fix this," and as he spoke, he made some ugly gashes across the pencil-portrait, and it greatly pleased the old lady.

"Do they live in a village?" asked Ralph.

"Yes, villages after their fashion," answered Mr. Arden. "Some of the Maoris have sheep-farms, and some are soldiers or sailors, or traders or mechanics, for they learn quite easily. They feel that they must yield before the English. They call the white man Pakéha, and they have this verse about him:

'As the Pakéha fly has driven out the Maori
　　fly,
As the Pakéha grass has killed the Maori grass,
As the Pakéha rat has slain the Maori rat,
As the Pakéha clover has starved the Maori
　　fern,
So will the Pakéha destroy the Maori.'

"They say of the advance of the English, 'Can you stay the surf which beats on Wanganui shore?'"

"They are brave men and good fighters," said Ralph, who was proud of the extensive knowledge of New Zealand affairs he had acquired.

"Oh, yes; we English know that," replied Mr. Arden readily.

"I'll tell you a good way to fix them!" How Rick's eyes snapped.

"You know — you know at home we had savages once; and a man was out chopping wood one day, and he saw Indians coming — so Nurse Fennel told me. He knew he must go with them as their prisoner, but he first asked a favor. He was splitting a log with a wedge, and would they just put their hands into the crack and help pull open the log? They were very willing, and put their — their hands in, and the man knocked the wedge out. Didn't they yell and kick!"

"Do you think that really happened, Rick?" asked the doctor.

"Well, Nurse Fennel said something like that did happen, and she wouldn't tell a lie."

After the return of the party to the *Antelope,* Rick thought that he had something of interest to say to Bumble-bee, the cook. He was absent from the sacred kitchen, and Rick smelling a nice, savory stew in the pot, ran a big long spoon down into it, and was ladling out a generous taste, when he heard steps. Looking up, he saw Bumble-bee coming.

"What yer-rup to here?" asked Bumble-bee.

Rick was silent, and clapped his spoon behind him.

"Ah, young man, I see de stew runnin' out ob dat spoon 'hind ye. Dat's allers de way. Wrong doin' leaves a tell-tale 'hind it. I'll forgib you, but nebber forget dat a wrong will leave a track 'hind it dat will show you up some day."

The moral was excellent, but Rick was too absorbed in watching Bumble-bee to think of anything else. Bumble-bee's eyes were rolling, and his face twisting into queer grimaces.

"Booh!" exclaimed Rick, when he was safe outside, "I know what Bumble-bee is; he's a Maori!"

CHAPTER XXXIII.

THROUGH COOK'S STRAIT.

ONE PROOF THAT THE EARTH IS ROUND.

SAILING away from Auckland, the *Antelope* was headed for Wellington, the capital of New Zealand; a handsome city on the southern shore of North Island. As they neared Wellington, Uncle Nat said to the boys:

"We are not only approaching the capital, but Port Nicholson also. I speak of it because I want to say something about the natives of this country. There have been wars between them and the English, and the land-question has been a bone of contention.

"In 1839 a vessel named the *Tory* arrived at Port Nicholson and a number of natives came on board. From the ship's deck various headlands, rivers and islands were pointed out, and the natives were asked if they would sell them. They said yes; and in less than three months a tract as big as Ireland was bought of the accommodating natives, and many chiefs signed papers of sale, but only few understood fully what they were doing. About nine thousand pounds were paid away

286

in goods. Some of the articles must have been extremely useful, as among them were sixty red night-caps, and twelve sticks of sealing wax, and twelve shaving brushes! If this is a specimen of the land transactions, we don't wonder that there has been trouble with the natives. There is only one safe way to proceed in this world, boys, and that is to be sure and *start right ;* then, you may go ahead."

The call of the *Antelope* at Wellington was very brief. A few goods were left and a few received, and two passengers came aboard. Then, the *Antelope* lifted her white antlers again and bounded away to sea. The passengers were ladies who had been teachers in New Zealand, but now wished to return to their homes in America, and for " variety's sake " preferred to go part of the way in a sailing vessel.

" What is the oldest one's name? " asked Rick.

" Wayland ; Miss Wayland, they call her," said Ralph.

" And I heard Miss Wayland call the other Lissa, and Uncle Nat called her also Miss Percy."

" Yes, Miss Lissa Percy or Miss Me-lissa Percy," said Ralph. " That's the way she writes her name, for I saw it on a card."

" Wouldn't it be funny if Uncle Nat should like Miss Wayland, and the doctor like Miss Lissa Percy? "

These gentlemen were both bachelors, and Rick's remark was quite a blow to Ralph who had already taken a fancy to Miss Lissa.

Uncle Nat quickly found out that they were singers. He was quite a musician himself, and he proposed the first evening of the voyage that they have a sing together out upon the deck. There stood Uncle Nat, playing away, his cheeks swollen to the size of small bellows. The first mate, Jenks, held the lantern. The doctor, Miss Wayland and Miss Lissa were looking over a sheet of music, while Gibbs, the second mate, stood in the rear and assisted in the singing.

"Let's have a song of home; 'Home Again,' say," said Uncle Nat.

"What's that?" thought Rick, who had retired to his elevated berth, but was now awakened by the singing, and so thrust down his head to ascertain the matter.

"What's that?" thought Ralph, who was in the lower berth; and running out his inquisitive head, he thrust it up excitedly. The two heads collided.

"Ow-w-w!" yelled Ralph.

"Ow-w-w!" yelled Rick.

No bumping, though, could destroy their curiosity, and slipping on their clothes they rushed eagerly out. Climbing up into the rigging, they looked down upon the singers.

"Ain't that nice, Rick. Miss Lissa is the best singer."

"No; I like Miss Wayland."

"She isn't."

"She is."

"Isn't" and "Is" came pretty near quarreling up there in the rigging, but the cessation of the singing removed the occasion of strife, and the boys went back to their berths.

Said Uncle Nat at the breakfast table, the next morning, "It would be nice to have a Mutual Improvement Society of some kind. Here are the boys, and if we could have something for them, I know it would work well; and it might instruct us all."

Everybody applauded the idea.

"What shall we call our society?" inquired Uncle Nat.

"Call it the Antelope Guild," said Miss Lissa, "as guilds are very fashionable."

Ralph thought this name was very sensible.

"All right," said Uncle Nat. "Perhaps Ralph will be secretary and put up notices."

A SONG OF HOME.

And Rick, what would he do? He fairly itched to help.

"I'll be — be 'saxton'!"

"Sexton?" said Miss Wayland; "I hope you don't want to bury us."

"I — I will fix the cabin, you know, and — and — "

"Oh, yes," said Uncle Nat, coming to Rick's help; "you can fix up the cabin and show the audience in, and so on."

That day there appeared on the outside of the cabin this notice:

Antelope Guild.

A meeting will be held to-morrow afternoon, in the cabin, at three o'clock, and a lecture will be given on Capt. Cook. Everybody cordially invited.

RALPH ROGERS, Secretary.

Underneath soon was seen this P. S. in another hand:

Seats provided for all. RICK ROGERS, "Saxton."

The ship was passing through Cook's Strait. It was a breezy day and the *Antelope* sprang from billow to billow, leaving a big print of foam wherever her feet touched the sea. The passengers gathered in the cabin, and the sailors were also invited to come. Jack Bobstay was off duty and was shown to a "front seat" by the "saxton." Siah was there, and so was Bumble-bee, who had washed up the dinner dishes in a hurry, and then spent a couple of hours bedecking himself. He came in a swallow-tail coat, and wore an enormous white bosom, "bearin' down upon the company like a whole flock of white sea-gulls," Jack Bobstay said.

Rick, Ralph and Siah were leaning over the edge of the table, their eyes intently fastened on the captain.

"Captain Cook!" said Uncle Nat, clearing his throat. "There are two things about Capt. Cook that it is worth while to remember" (here Uncle Nat looked down into the shining eyes of the young auditors): "One of the two things is that Capt. Cook rose from a humble place to be the able man he really was. In the year 1745, as I make it out, a young fellow stepped on board an English collier at Whitby, and asked for a position as cabin boy. Depend upon it, there were some hard things and some menial things to be done, but you all know there is a chance to get up from the hold of a ship to the mast-head, if one is willing to climb; and so it is about the positions in all sea-service. James Cook was the one to climb. I imagine that he was no loafer; that he was prompt and obedient, and that he was just the one to be thoughtful and studious. Such a boy watching the tops of the ships go down at sea, would be likely to infer it was one proof that the world was round. I can easily imagine James Cook to be that kind of a thinking lad. The cabin boy began to go up. He became a mate and then a master.

"In 1755, Cook entered the royal navy, still climbing up, climbing up, just as when he was on board a collier. He was finally appointed to the frigate *Mercury*, a vessel that took part in the expedition of Gen. Wolfe to Quebec — is there a boy here who has not read that story? James Cook piloted the fleet up the St. Lawrence, making soundings, and setting buoys. He led the boats of the fleet to the attack upon the French, and saw that the soldiers were successfully landed.

"Another thing for us all to remember is that James Cook never felt that he was too old to learn. Stepping to a higher position, promoted to the *Northumberland* flag-ship, how did he spend his leisure time — smoking a dirty pipe, and sipping grog? Look into the cabin of the *Northumberland*. There he is, bending over books on mathematics and astronomy. One who studies about the sea, cannot well dispense with a knowledge of the heavenly bodies. Take that question of the tides: It is thought that the moon attracts and raises the water, producing high tide, and when the sun and moon draw together — for the sun has an **influence on** the water — then we have our highest or spring tides —

the lowest be-
ing called neap-
tides, when sun
and moon do
not pull togeth-
er. This is all
based on the
principle that
one mass of
matter will at-
tract another.
The tides are
an illustration
of the connec-
t i o n between
studies of the
sea and astron-
omy. C o o k
studied the sub-
ject of the hea-
v e n l y bodies.
He made such
able observa-
tions o n a n
eclipse ·of the
sun that he be-
came a marked

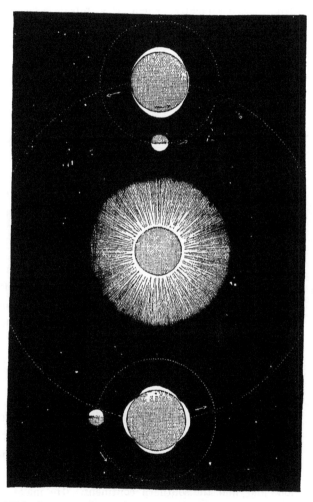

man. He also published a number of very valuable charts.

"Boys may think of Capt. Cook as only a kind of rough-and-ready man, hot for adventure, but he was really a student and a man of science. Consequently, when the Royal Society wished to obtain observations on the passage of the planet Venus across the face of the sun, Cook was picked out as the man to command a vessel that would go to the Pacific ocean and visit parts favorable to an observation of the sun. He sailed from Plymouth, England, in 1768. He ac-quitted himself with great credit in that voyage. About this time men were talking over the point, is there not some great southern continent? I suppose they thought the world might lose its balance if there were not something away down here at the south to balance the heavy lands at the north.

"After Capt. Cook and his companions - had looked at the sun all they cared to, they continued their voyage and came down here to find a southern continent. Then it was that Capt. Cook visited New Zealand, that had not had a visit from a European for over a hundred years. He saw first this strait we are now sailing through. He did not receive a very cordial welcome from the natives of New Zealand, and it fearfully astonished them when one of their number dropped dead at the firing of a musket by an officer of Capt. Cook. Fire-arms puzzled them.

"Capt. Cook visited Australia in 1770, examined a long piece of its coast, and claimed it for Great Britain. He sailed on, meeting with various adventures, reaching England once more. The keel of his ship had made a furrow of foam all round the world, but it took three years to do it. Yet people were not satisfied; and to learn finally if there might be a southern continent, Capt. Cook was sent once more, when forty-four years old, to circumnavigate the globe and find the southern continent. He made new discoveries, and his two ships sailed over sixty thousand miles; but they did not find the big southern land that was anticipated. In all that long voyage, so good was his management that Capt. Cook lost but one man by sickness, and not even a spar of any special worth. The cabin boy was now a famous man. He kept studying, however, for though

IN COOK'S STRAIT.

one may be wiser than a whole family of owls, still there is always something to learn.

"In 1776, he received a gold medal for a valuable essay. People, you know, must always have a hobby. They now began to ask whether they might not get to Asia by sailing to the northwest, and Capt. Cook was thought to be the man to find out. The summer our country declared its independence — when was that, boys?"

"1776," said Ralph promptly.

"The summer of '76, Capt. Cook sailed away again. I wonder if

he thought he might never come back. He sailed away, resolved to pierce the ice-land by way of Behring's straits. He made a faithful trial, but Jack Frost finally drove him back. That was in 1778, and Capt. Cook named the point he succeeded in reaching, Joy Cape. In the course of this voyage,

"WISER THAN A WHOLE FAMILY OF OWLS."

he had discovered the Sandwich Islands, and he now turned back to these; not to give up his attempt however, but only to get ready for another northern voyage, which was like the cabin boy of old days, who was bound to win if he could. He discovered a new island, Hawaii. The inhabitants were thievish, and stole one of Capt. Cook's boats. The captain naturally wished to get his own back again, and concluded to steal their king, and then exchange a king for a boat, which was doubtless all he was worth; but the course pursued was a mistaken one. I do not believe in deceit. But the captain went ashore and urged the king to visit his ship. The people suspected the captain's motive, and urged the king not to go. The two parties began to quarrel. Capt. Cook insisted on taking the king, and the strife became violent. The English discharged their muskets in response to a shower of stones from the natives. Capt. Cook's men escaped to their boats, and as the captain also turned he was severely struck, and fell into the water, his face downwards. Like tigers, the savages fell upon him, trampling him down until dead. His body was terribly mutilated, and only the bones could be found when his men afterwards came ashore and by violence wrested the remains from the savages' possession. In the blue sea he loved so fondly and sailed so persistently, they laid away all that was left of the famous mariner. You will find traces of him all over these Pacific seas.

" In New Zealand, down to the year 1836, the story of Capt. Cook's visit was preserved among the natives. They told Mr. Polack that their fathers took the captain's ship 'at first for a gigantic bird, and were struck with the beauty and size of its wings, as they supposed the sails to be. But on seeing a smaller bird, unfledged, descending into the water, and a number of parti-colored beings, apparently in human shape, the bird was regarded as a houseful of divinities.' They were very much astonished. Then, too, the death of one of their number, killed by a musket, and a great fighting man among them, was a deep mystery. How could they obtain revenge on divinities that could kill them at a distance ?

" Capt. Cook will long be remembered as a daring navigator : A a man who climbed up high from a low round on the ladder. Let not the boys here forget him."

Ralph, Rick and Siah drew a long breath. The story had intensely interested them. Each one resolved to see how high he could mount in life. Siah, that night in his dreams, was continually rising up and bumping his head against the low ceiling above his berth. In disgust, he ceased at last, and fell back into deep unbroken slumbers. The doctor declared the next morning that the ambitious spirit of the Pacific navigator had pervaded all living things on board the

Antelope.   He asserted that in a dream he had seen one of the roosters in the hen-coops marching out upon the deck, there to inveigle a crew of timorous rats into his service.   The captain's flat cap had been appropriated by this aspiring rooster, and he was strutting about proudly.   The doctor also thought it was not safe to remain on board a ship whose crew in the night might be over-powered by such a band of mutinous as well as ambitious beings.

CHAPTER XXXIV.

AUSTRALIA, BY RICK ROGERS.

A SOURCE OF AUSTRALIAN WEALTH.

"YOU won't see Middle Island, that is, to visit it, boys," said Jack Bobstay, one day.

"No," said Rick and Ralph, their inquisitive natures anxious to see everything possible.

"Stewart's Island is a small affair, but Middle Island, or South, as it is sometimes called, is worth seeing. It is over five hundred miles long, boys. It has some splendid mountains — tall, I tell ye. Mt. Cook is about thirteen thousand feet. There are some lively towns, too, in Middle Island; not equal to North Island, it is true, but very, very respectable, for I have been there, boys. And they have gold mines. I was in the scramble that put for the gold in New Zealand. Lots of gold there. But I expect — I expect we shall have something fine to-morrow, much better than any of my talk. And here is the notice, now, in as good style as a .commodore's order to his fleet. Read it, Ralph."

"There will be a meeting of the *Antelope Guild* to-morrow afternoon, to listen to the distinguished Sir Richard Rogers, from Concord, Mass.

"RALPH ROGERS, *Secretary*."

The "distinguished lecturer" was so prominently mentioned that the "saxton" did not feel like attaching his signature.

The *Antelope Guild* turned out in strong force to hear a lecture on Australia.

"You must not expect much from me," pleaded Rick, his eyes twinkling, " 'cause — 'cause, you know, I'm not used to it; but I'll do the best I can."

With a round of applause, the fraternity encouraged their modest brother to go on.

"Australia is the biggest island anywhere about. It is about two thousand miles wide, at its widest part, and its greatest length is twenty-four hundred miles. It has three millions of square miles. You could cut off a piece of Australia big as Great Britain and Ireland, and then there would be enough left for twenty-five slices just like it. It is only one-fifth smaller than the continent of Europe. If you leave out Alaska, the United States and Australia are of about the same bigness.

"In Australia are Western Australia, South Australia, Queensland, New South Wales and Victoria. The English own Australia, but they let the people do about as they please. Jack Bobstay says that Uncle Sam is thought a good deal of out this way, and uncle is going to annex Japan and Australia. The outside of Australia, along the sea, is quite nice, but away in, the land is pretty rocky and sandy and dry. They say the inside pans out better, the more it is known. Dutch sailors came pretty often to Australia, a long time ago, but Capt. Cook, who was smarter than all of them, came in 1770, and hoisted the British flag over New South Wales.

"The convicts came here first in 1788, but that was stopped after a while, and a better class of people came. There are now not far from three millions of people here. The people that lived here first, the savages, do not amount to much, and are not as smart as the Maoris.

Australia sends out to other people more gold and wool than anything else. In Victoria alone, one billion of gold dollars has been taken out of the earth, and if you count New Zealand and Tasmania, there are between sixty and seventy million sheep, owned by the people this way; enough to stock a small farm. They have coal and railroads and the telegraph in Australia, and all they need to make¯them become a very great people is to become a part of the United States, and then be annexed to Concord."

Amid the patriotic applause of the *Guild*, the speaker ceased.

" Australia is a singular place," observed Uncle Nat. " She is queer for her very size as an island, being so very big. She is queer for her immense sheep-farms; queer for her gold mines; queer for her animals, and queer for almost everything."

" There are two great seasons in Australia: the wet and the dry. Sometimes it is pretty hot, and fierce wind and dust storms rage; every climate, though, has its disadvantages as well as its advantages.

" There is a big island north of Australia that I wish the boys could see— New Guinea. Its mountains are wild, and the people are savages; but the soil is rich, and the climate temperate, and some day New Guinea will be heard from. Colonists are sure to go there. Then there is Tasmania, south of Australia, an island about three quarters as large as Ireland; one hundred and seventy miles long, and one hundred and sixty miles wide. It is fertile in soil, and not severe in climate. Convicts were sent there once, but this has stopped now, and a better class of residents go there. Its capital is Hobart Town, and the place is an enterprising one. Well, if we do not see these places, there will be enough for us to look at in Australia, and we will make for Sydney fast as possible."

CHAPTER XXXVI.

SYDNEY.

THE CALM OF SUNSET.

IT was toward the close of the day when the *Antelope* sailed into Port Jackson, the body of water leading to the city of Sydney. The sun was rapidly sinking toward the horizon, hanging up all sorts of cloud-fabrics in the west, gay as the Christmas display that a dry-goods dealer makes in his windows. Uneasy waters were subsiding for the night, and near the shore there were surfaces as smooth and glistening as gray polished steel. The shining waters of the harbor widened on either hand. The land sloped down to the water, jutting out in points and making charming little nooks where pretty villages were cradled. From one of these villages a steamer was shooting away, its bow headed for the city that is four miles from the ocean.

"How calm it is getting to be, Doctor Walton," said Rick as he watched the water.

"Yes; it would seem as if sunset ought to bring calm. We are thinking then of rest."

"Sydney is the oldest city in Australia," said the doctor to the boys.

"The very first settlement?" inquired Ralph.

"Let me explain. When the British government knew it could not use the American colonies as a kind of sewer into which to drain the bad blood of its society, that is to say, their convicts, they thought

of Australia as a sewer; and as Capt. Cook had brought a good report from Botany Bay, not far from here, it was determined to send a batch of prisoners to that spot. And do you know why it was called Botany Bay?"

"I do," said Ralph; "for I read about it the other day. It was so called on account of the many flowers found in that neighborhood by a botanist, Mr. Banks."

"Yes, that is it. Well, when the attempt was made to occupy Botany Bay, the place did not seem the best for a settlement, and they weighed anchor and came up here with their convicts and started a town. Over fifty years the convicts were sent here, but the custom was stopped at last; and when they tried in England to send others — that was in 1849 — Sydney stood right up and said no. It has become a large and populous city, and must have at least one hundred and ten thousand inhabitants; and in the suburbs, our pilot told me, there are over ninety thousand more."

The next morning Ralph Rogers was leaning over the ship's rail, looking down upon the waters of Sydney Harbor. There was a sail stretched overhead, "jest to dry and take out Neptune's tears," Jack Bobstay said. At Ralph's right was a string of fish caught that morning. At his left was a dog that had planted two paws on the ship's rail, his outstretched tongue giving him a look of desire to say something social, if he only could. It was a strange dog that had come aboard that morning, and Ralph had nicknamed him "Paws." Ralph, though, was not thinking of the water below, the fishing-line in his hand, or the dog at his side. He was taking comfort in the thought that he and Rick and Siah and Jack Bobstay were going off on a "cruise" through Sydney.

"Take care of the boys," said Uncle Nat as they were about leaving the ship.

"Aye, aye, sir;" responded Jack.   "I'll have an eye out for 'em :
two eyes even."

"And Paws may come.   Paws, good fellow, come here!" cried Ralph.

RALPH LEANING OVER THE SHIP'S RAIL.

The four-footed creature gave his hand a brush with his tongue,
and it was anything but a dry lick.

"We will go into one of the crack streets," said Jack, "and I guess I can find it, though things have changed since I was here."

"Sydney makes me think of Boston, Mr. Bobstay," said Ralph.

"Does it? Well, here is George street. See the buildings of stone."

"It is a nice street; doesn't it go through the whole length of the city? The pilot told the doctor so."

"Yes; and we will go into Pitt street next."

They found banks and newspaper offices, and a variety of business-quarters of importance. Looking along Market street, Rick saw foliage ahead:

"Oh - h - h! I guess there is a garden," he shouted.

It was "Hyde Park," a pretty spot containing forty acres, and here was a statue of "Albert the Good," and one also of Capt. Cock.

"More trees!" shouted Siah, later in the day.

They had reached another park, the "Domain," inclosing one hundred and thirty-eight acres, and leading to the bright clear water at Farm Cove.

"And something else is here, boys," called out Jack. He was pointing at the Botanical Gardens, green with a variety of strange growths amassed there. During the day Jack showed the boys some of the institutions of Sydney, and among them were the University, Government House, and Garden Palace.

CHAPTER XXXVI.

THE STORM.

"GLORIOUS" TO BE A SAILOR.

"BOUN' for Melbourne, boys!"

"Where did you say we are going, Siah?" asked Ralph.

"Melbourne."

"Will it take long?" asked Rick.

"Dun know, chile. We shall find out by the time we get there."

They were sailing along when Jack Bobstay's announcement to Rick was, "It's coming!"

"What's coming?"

"A sou'easter. Don't you see that the wind is risin'? And those clouds way off are goin' to pour buckets, I know, and the sea is getting to be uneasy."

Rick thought on the banks of the Concord River that it must be nice to be a sailor, and he had pictured himself on board a ship, sporting a trim, neat, sailor's rig, wearing a big white collar and big black bow, and it did seem "glorious." But he had been changing his opinion. He had been rather skeptical on the point that very day. He noticed that the ship was getting to be quite unsteady, as he started from Bumble-bee's quarters, carrying a plate of soup in his h a n d s. The deck had been washed that morning and was still wet, and it required careful steering on the part of the Concord navigator to reach without accident the cabin-door.

"Glad I'm not a sailor," thought Rick, "and won't have to furl a sail up on the yard."

By twilight wind, rain and sea were after the *Antelope*. Old Bumble-bee put his head in at the cabin-door, and his body quickly followed. He brought a portion of the supper with which he had started from his domain.

"Mos' los' your supper, ladies and genmen, comin' across dat deck! De sea is runnin' high," he said.

Uncle Nat was out on deck giving orders for the trimming

TRYING TO CARRY A PLATE OF SOUP.

of the ship. He brought word the latter part of the evening that Jack Bobstay's story was that the "for'castle was flooded with water."

That night was an anxious one. The ladies retired to their state-room at an early hour, and then the doctor went to his, and Rick and Ralph stole off to theirs. The boys could not sleep. The thumping of the w a v e s against the ship, the roar of the wind, the cries of the officers on deck, made a dismal medley.

NOT SO "GLORIOUS" TO BE A SAILOR.

"I don't want to be a sailor," said Rick.

"Nor I," said Ralph, tumbling now into Rick's berth, declaring that he wanted company.

"I hope we won't get near the shore and go on to the rocks," groaned Rick.

"I wish I was in Concord," thought Ralph.

"Let's get into Uncle Nat's berth, Ralph, quick as we can put."

"Come on."

Two figures in white made their way through the dimly-lighted cabin, bruising their shins against pieces of overturned furniture, and as they were crawling into Uncle Nat's berth, the ship gave a sudden lurch and in went the boys all in a heap! It was a heap that was very much "mixed up"

"What's here?" said Uncle Nat, hurrying into his state-room, and swinging a lantern over the heap in his berth. "A regular puddin', all lumped together! Well, boys, stay here, and don't worry. Remember that Uncle Nat is round!"

"And there is Somebody else round," whispered Rick. " Let's say our prayers over again."

Trembling young mariners! How they wished they were saying them beside a certain little bed in Concord.

Rick at last had so many " sticks " in his eyes that he dropped

AFTER THE STORM.

into a slumber; Ralph, though, kept awake, listening to the wind and the crash of the waves. Toward morning, there came a heavier sea forcing its way into the after-house. Creeping to the door of the state-room, Ralph saw the water splashing across the cabin-floor and creating an ugly panic. Uncle Nat here rushed in, the water dripping profusely from his oil-cloth suit.

"All right here," he sang out. "Ah, Ralph! And the doctor and the ladies?"

"O captain! What, shall we do in this terrible storm?" screamed a female voice from a state-room.

"Still alive!" shouted the doctor, thrusting his head forward.

"Oh, we shall weather it! Don't be afraid, ladies!" cheerily cried Uncle Nat. "Where's Rick?"

Rick could answer for himself, as he was now awake, and Uncle Nat going to his berth held up his lantern, and by its light saw a pale little face in among the bed-clothes.

"I was trying, uncle, to say: ' 'Twas midnight on the waters.' "

"Well, that's good; I didn't know but what I might have to say that or something else like it, on the waters themselves, Rick, for that last big wave almost swept me into the sea. I happened to put my hand out, and caught a ring-bolt, and that saved me. You want to tell me something, Rick? What is it? 'Put my head lower?' Now tell me!"

"I have prayed for you, uncle," whispered Rick.

"Dear little suppliant! I guess we will come out all right, for the rain has been holding up, and our blow can't last always."

He left the boys and went out again. When it was light enough to see anything distinctly, Rick put his head out of the cabin-door. The sea was rolling up in every direction into hills — "ten thousand of them," said Rick; and these only curled over and fell in ten thousand shattering, foaming cascades. In the midst of this green and white whirl, this anger and froth and tumult, rocked the *Antelope*, insignificant as a straw on the surface of a spring-freshet. Rick drew in his head, and concluded that he did not care to cultivate the sea for a living. But storms do not rage forever. All that day the wind was lessening its violence. The waves began to lower. Overhead, there were grayish rents in the black heavens. Finally, there was peace, and white summer-clouds tufted the sky. When the sea had gone down, and the vast waters swept away unruffled, then Rick said: "I guess I would like to be a sailor."

The wind was again blowing in the direction of Melbourne, and the *Antelope* raced along rapidly. As the days went by, her white antlers were seen in Port Philip Bay, then in Hobson's Bay, finally halting at Hobson's Bay Railway Pier.

HOBSON'S BAY RAILWAY PIER.

315

" The port of Melbourne is two and a half miles from the city, though the Yarra-Yarra river, boys, flows up to Melbourne, and smaller vessels go there ; but we stop here," said Uncle Nat.

"What is the name of Melbourne's port?" asked Ralph.

" Sandridge."

It was now December, 1880, and Uncle Nat had told the boys they should have an opportunity to see Australia's International Exhibition at Melbourne. Uncle Nat's movements were delayed, but he told Bumble-bee, who was going to the city, that he might take the boys with him, and give them a look at the exhibition.

" 'Fraid now, cap'n, I couldn't manage both in a crowd ; but I might take jest one — Rick, say," replied Bumble-bee.

Rick was getting to be a favorite with Bumble-bee ; a rather singular thing, for Bumble-bee was reckoned an enemy to boys in general.

" He's pert, and sometimes can be sassy," soliloquized the old cook, explaining the matter to himself ; " but den he's a heap smart, and I see a zemblance between him and my grandson, Nebuchadnezzar."

Nebuchadnezzar was a colored young citizen of Charlestown, Mass., and the " zemblance " between him and Rick. Old Bumble-bee had suggested to Jack Bobstay. Jack could not appreciate it.

" Oh, it's not so much de — de features," explained Old Bumble-bee, " but it's de 'spression."

" Yes," said Jack, " it must be that ; " for he had puzzled his brains over the problem of the " zemblance."

Bumble-bee and Rick took the cars at Sandridge for Melbourne.

Alighting at the city station they found themselves in a crowd, all bound for the Great Exhibition.

" Honey," said the cook, " you jes' grip me 'hind, takin' hold good, an' we'll go froo dis yer crowd in less dan no time."

"I've got hold," exclaimed Rick, seizing Bumble-bee's coat-tails.

" Hold good, fur I wouldn't drop ye fur de world, sartin; but I want both hands, chile."

In his younger days the cook had been an adept in the paddling of a boat, and it had impressed a peculiar movement upon his arms when walking — for they had a swing, as if he were paddling still. There

BOURKE STREET, MELBOURNE, 1880, LOOKING EAST.

was a sinister design now in the soul of Bumble-bee; for putting out his arms he gave a sweep with them, as if Rick were a boat just behind, and somehow must be paddled along, and all obstacles must be pressed aside.

"Hold on dar! Got a sure grip, honey?" shouted the cook.

"Aye, aye, sir," sang out Rick.

The people laughed to see this big colored man paddling ahead, in his wake a grinning little boy that clung to his coat-tails.

"Oh, I tell you, Ralph," said Rick that night, "it was fun; and

Bumble-bee went right ahead, geeing this way, and geeing that. We made real good time, and we got into another crowd too, before the day was over. We were on Bourke street — a nice street, Ralph; some real nice buildings there, and lots of carriages were in the street, and in one place the people on the sidewalk were as thick as bees; but we went right straight through them! I felt as if I was on a train of cars."

"I call you de Annex," said Bumble-bee, looking round and grinning.

When Bumble-bee and the "Annex" were clear of the first crowd that we described, Rick looked about him. He noticed how straight the streets were, and that the intersecting ones crossed at right angles.

"It makes me think of Philadelphy," observed Bumble-bee.

The streets were broad as well as straight.

"They hab sumfin' to 'blow' about here in Melbourne," said Bumble-bee, noticing the enterprising aspect of the city, and using a popular Australian phrase (known elsewhere, also). "We'll hunt up dat Great Internal Exhibition fust, you know, honey," continued Bumble-bee.

They found it in Carlton Gardens. The buildings, which cost about one million two hundred and fifty thousand dollars, covered five and a half acres of ground. The main building, shaped like a cross, was five hundred feet long, traversed by a transept two hundred and seventy feet deep. The dome rose at the intersection of the nave and transept, and reached an altitude of two hundred and twenty-three feet. Its great height made it a landmark for miles around. The grounds were decorated with flowers, and everywhere wore the beauty of summer, while fountains gracefully threw into the air their crystal streams. Bumble-bee and Rick wandered about, drifting with the throng that surged forward and backward. Many nations were interested in the exhibition, and contributed generously. There were all kinds of goods, machinery and productions. After a while they came to the department of the United States. As Old Bumble-bee surveyed its display, he swelled with that secret convic. tion, " I am an American citizen."

" Come here, honey," he whispered to Rick. They retired to a secluded nook behind a barricade of goods. There the loyal old heart whispered : " Now, chile, let's gib free sheers for de Stars and Stripes ; sort ob easy, ye know — whisper-like."

And there in the dusky corner, Bumble-bee and his ward cheered " sort-ob-easy " for the dear old flag.

"Bress him !" thought Bumble-bee. " He does look so much like my Nebuchadnezzar."

THE PUBLIC MUSEUM AND LIBRARY.

They visited one other noteworthy place that day ; Melbourne's public museum and library.

" I'm so much interested in de cause ob ed-di-fication," said Bumble- bee, " dat I must see dis."

"I WONDER WHICH WAY HOME IS?"

CHAPTER XXXVII.

"GOLD! GOLD!"

UNCLE Nat had taken the boys to the sea-shore and Rick had improved the first opportunity that offered to occupy a sand-hummock, and, bare-headed and bare-footed, he looked off upon the waters sweeping away to the blue, misty line of the horizon. He was talking to himself:

"Uncle Nat says we are going to leave soon. He wants to show us a sheep-farm and some gold-mines, and then we are going to China. I wonder which way home is!"

There he reclined, watching the birds in their flight, a distant sail, and the wide, level sea. He rose finally and began to hunt ·for Ralph, soon finding him.

"Ralph, where is Ballaarat? Uncle Nat says he is to take us up there to see the gold mines."

"Oh," exclaimed Ralph, disliking to confess that he knew as little about Ballaarat as Rick; "Bal — Balrat is — "

"Ballaa-rat," interrupted Rick. "That is the way!"

"Well, what difference does it make what kind of rat it is? It is up in the country somewhere — a country-rat; and it must be worth seeing."

Having received this important information, Rick began to think over various preparations for the trip. "A bag I must have ready, 'cause if I should find any gold lying round loose I should want something in which to put it. Wouldn't it be nice to get it full? And to-morrow we start. Good!"

To-morrow came fast enough, at least for Uncle Nat who was busy with all kinds of work. He found time in the morning, though, to show his inquisitive nephews the beautiful Government House, whose tower rises up into the air one hundred and forty-five feet. From its top there is a far-reaching, magnificent view. After this visit, Uncle Nat and the boys took the cars for Ballaarat.

"Who's that?" whispered Rick to Uncle Nat, as they looked out of the car window. It was a dark-faced, thick-haired, roughly-dressed sort of a savage that they saw.

"That's one of the natives of the country. I'll hunt up a picture of them when I can."

That day the boys saw a picture of the natives of Australia. There were about twenty in the group. They had dark faces, an abundance of black hair, wide mouths, flat noses, sharp little eyes, and, as Ralph said, were "clothed variously." One at least sported a shirt-collar, and three wore hats or caps.

"They like to live out-doors in summer," said Uncle Nat, "and in

rough weather, live or stay in bark huts. On the sea-shore they have bark canoes for their fishing. They don't like steady work, their ideas of religion are low, and they would make good Mormans if they were in Salt Lake City, judging by the number of wives the men like to have."

We return to the ride in the cars.

"Now, boys, I will tell you about the finding of gold in Australia," said Uncle Nat. "Gold was first found in a little stream called Summerhill Creek, in New South Wales. That was in May, 1851. The next month it was found in Ballaarat, Victoria. When it was known, a furious rush for the gold-country began. They came flocking to Ballaarat at the rate of five hundred a day. The shearer quit his sheep and the house-servant left the kitchen. Policemen had no further use for their badges and sailors forsook their ships. Everybody was going to the gold-diggings. Of course no houses were there, and so there were streets of canvas tents. But very naturally, the question came up, 'Who owns the gold?' Could a man stick in his pick wherever he pleased? Government said a miner must pay thirty shillings a month for the privilege of digging, and then the tax was raised to three pounds a month. It was difficult for government to collect the tax, as the miners hated it; and some refused to pay. At Ballaarat there was so much trouble that, the miners having fortified a certain position, an attack was made upon them at night, and thirty or forty of the miners were killed. But things quieted down at last. Gold has now been found in Sandhurst and other places. It is said that in Victoria one-third of the soil is considered to be gold-bearing."

When the boys alighted at Ballaarat, Rick expected to see a string of canvas tents and run into a lot of miners carrying picks on their shoulders and shovels in their hands; a wild, rough country all about them. He hoped, too, he might see a piece of shining gold sticking out of the soil that would be prey for his bag.   Instead, he saw a city.   There were houses, stores, banks, churches, schools and public gardens.

Rick was disappointed, and took little interest in the fact that a gentleman was detailing to Uncle Nat that Ballaarat had not far from fifty thousand people.

"Come, boys, we are going to visit a gold mine," called out Uncle Nat.   He had hired a team, and off they rattled.

"Good!" thought Rick.   "There may be a chance for my bag, and I'll take Bumble-bee one piece of gold, sure."

First, the boys saw a hole in the ground, and an iron box or cage waiting to lower them — somewhere.   They went down, down, down, and then stopped.   There Rick saw a horse harnessed into a truck resting on a railway.   Mounting the truck they were steadily pulled through a long, damp, dark passage.

"I rode along for a quarter of a mile in one of these underground holes once," said Uncle Nat, "and then climbing a ladder twenty-five feet high, we came to another hole traversed by a track.   Running out of this second tunnel were side-passages, and in these miners were at work."

"I shall be glad when we get to the end of this kind of travel," said Ralph.

They reached the end and then the manager of the mine who had come with Uncle Nat, said they were inspecting "alluvial grit."

"What alluvial grit is," said Uncle Nat, "please tell these wide-awake boys, who would like to know about it."

"It is earth washed down by a stream, and gold may be in it.   Swept this way by the water, it has lodged here.   See, all covered up under the ground!   We dig for and find it."

The manager took a light and held it over the earth.

"Do you see the bits of gold — the tiny little specks there?"

"Oh-h-h!" said the boys, with an affirmative tone.

There it was, flashing like very minute stars out of a very dingy heaven. Rick wanted to pick up a memento for Bumble-bee, but he restrained himself.

"Now if you will come back with me," said the manager, "I will show you what we do with the dirt."

Riding back and riding up again, they were glad to leave the darkness and dampness behind them, though Rick said he was "sorry to leave the poor miners boxed up down-stairs." A call came for somebody!

The manager stopped and listened. "I am very sorry, friends," he said, "but I must leave you."

When he had gone, Uncle Nat said: "Well, boys, we, too, ought to be going, but I can tell you something, for I have been here before and seen the gold-dirt puddled or mixed with water. The earth was put in a trough and water poured in. I was on a platform at the top of the machinery, and saw that the matter in the trough was worked by something like a harrow. The water and mud ran off, and the weight of the gold and any refuse carried it to the bottom. Water was again poured in with the gold, a man working it all over, the gold once more sinking to the bottom, the stones and mud passing off. When the gold had been separated, it was gathered up and put into earthen pots. It was then melted, poured into molds, washed, and sent off to the bank."

"But, uncle," inquired Ralph, "I thought there were quartz-crushers."

"So there are, for they take out a good deal of quartz also in Australia. I guess we must stop to see the crushing."

Another mine was visited. Here, the gold was found in quartz. A quantity had been brought to the surface, and a workman explained

to Uncle Nat and the boys the process of quartz-crushing:
" There, here is machinery for breaking up the rock taken from the
mine. We use stampers, as we call them, and they are worked
by steam. The quartz is thrown under the stampers and these break
the quartz into a powder in the midst of a current of water. By
that current the powder is swept away and carried over quicksilver,
which collects the gold. Then we place this in a retort, and separate
the gold. Perhaps these young gentlemen would like to carry off a
little memento of the quartz."

The young gentlemen were very happy to do so. While Siah, Jack
Bobstay, the doctor and the ladies were remembered, it was a relief to
Rick to be able to carry home a specimen to the dusky monarch of the
ship's kitchen.

CHAPTER XXXVIII.

A BIG SHEEP FARM.

A DOG RAN UP AND BARKED AT THEM.

"BAH! bah!" went Rick one morning.

"Bah! bah!" was Ralph's echoing cry.

"That means," exclaimed Uncle Nat, "that you are expecting to start for that big sheep farm to-day, and we will go as soon as you are ready. We have a long ride in the cars, and then another piece to travel by horse-power, and it will take us the most of three days. An old friend, Mr. Bright, will then meet us and take us in his team."

The journey was continued as planned, and Mr. Bright met them at the appointed place. He was a broad-shouldered, full-bearded man, his face and hands well tanned by exposure to the sun, his manner very energetic, and his whole air that of a person to whom in an emergency you would be likely to run, and he would work for you ; and yet if you were a servant in his employ, he would very quickly set you to work for him. He wore a felt hat with a broad, slouching brim, and he carried in his hand a horse-whip. Behind him, patiently stood two big dogs that he afterwards designated as "Tom and Jim, my favorites."

Mr. Bright was very cordial, and he advanced, holding out a plump, sun-baked hand.

"Halloo, cap'n! Welcome to the bush! I am glad to see you! How — how d'ye do ?" and he griped Uncle Nat's hand with unmistakable heartiness. Then came an energetic discharge of questions, flying at the captain in quick succession, like revolver-shots. He could only pick up the first shot and reply to that.

"Oh, thank you, Sam, I am well. These are my nephews, who want to see what the bush is and how sheep in the bush look."

"Well, they are entirely welcome, and I'll take the best care of 'em, see if I don't."

"Isn't he splendid, Rick ? " whispered Ralph.

"He's big, Ralph."

"Now we are going to ride off into the bush, boys," said Mr. Bright.

"What is the bush ? " asked Ralph. "Is it where bushes grow ? "

"Ha, ha! Pretty big bushes! Let me say that the lands mostly occupied in Australia are wood-land, though our people have occupied some plains. There are the Darling Downs in our country, immense prairies, level, and more like prairies in the United States. About the second week in September they are just one sea of green. They are splendid plains, and the sheep occupy them for grazing. The most of the country, though, that is occupied is woodland, and there are two names for it ; scrub and bush. When the undergrowth is very close and thick and tangled, so that you must fight your way ahead, axe in hand, we call it 'scrub.' When there is not much undergrowth and the trees are sort of open, and a man on horseback can get comfortably through the woods, then we

PRIZE AUSTRALIAN SHEEP.

call it the 'bush.' You have been riding in the bush already a long time."

As Mr. Bright said, they had for a long time been riding in the bush. They had been journeying among trees, trees, trees. Australian scenery is peculiar. The woodland is generally more like a park of trees than a dense forest. The traveller does not often meet with patches or streams of water, to vary and brighten the landscape ; but his journey is through forest after forest.

" What are these trees ? " asked Ralph.

" The bush is of the gum-tree growth," said Mr. Bright. " Botanists call it the eucalyptus, but we common folks say gum-tree. There are a good many kinds in all Australia. Sometimes it grows very big. I have seen a gum-tree that measured sixteen feet through the trunk, and one tree I heard of had run up to the height of four hundred and eighty feet ! Why, they say a plank one hundred and forty-eight feet long has been sawed out of a gum-tree. When so very tall, running up straight, without branches for a long way, they are handsome as pillars in a church. "

" Why do they call them gum-trees ? " asked Rick.

" Because a kind of gum escapes from the tree. There is one kind that the natives use as food, and another serves as a medicine, and a third, when tapped, gives out a juice from which a kind of beer has been made ; and that, I think, they might as well let alone."

" Oh, Ralph, what is that ? A 'possum, I guess. Bumble-bee says he would give anything to see one."

" Where is it, Rick ? " asked Mr. Bright.

" There, that dark thing in the bush," answered Rick, anxious to show off his familiarity with Australian phraseology..

" Oh ! " laughed Mr. Bright. " That creature ? That is a kangaroo."

" He doesn't seem to be frightened."

" Why should he be ? You could not catch him."

" There are two or three of them. Let's chase them."

" Do you want to try it, Rick ? "

" Oh, yes."

Mr. Bright kindly pulled in his horses, and they all jumped out and together made for the kangaroos. These looked about, as if stupidly wondering what these folks were up to, and then giving several tremendous leaps, they bounded away in a style that mocked all would-be pursuers, and were lost among the gum-trees. The ride was resumed.

"Trees, trees, trees!" said Uncle Nat.

"Yes, but in a couple of hours you will see something beside bush," replied his host.

At the end of two hours, Uncle Nat looking up, saw a — house!

"What's that, Sam?"

"That? It looks like a house, doesn't it? That is our stopping-place."

"Your place?"

"Yes, it must be mine, for it belongs to no one else."

It was a two-story house, a veranda bordering the front side. Back of it, and on either side, were grouped various buildings; a kitchen, house for servants, stable and carriage-house.

Mr. Bright's wife, a young woman in a blue dress, her arms full of a fat baby, came out to the veranda and welcomed them.

"There will be time before dark," said Mr. Bright, "to take a stroll on my place, if you would like to go. We will have something to eat, though, first."

After a lunch, Mr. Bright took his visitors out-doors again.

"There," he said, looking about him, "this is my home-paddock, and by that the boys will understand just an enclosure. I may have about sixty acres here. It is all fenced in quite securely, and it gives my horses a chance to run about; and to catch the four or five that are loose, I keep one in the stable. These are for personal or home use. Now we will cross this paddock, and just beyond comes a second, that may enclose three hundred acres, and I keep my working horses here; about thirty. Next to this is my wool-shed paddock; and halloo! there is a sign of it among those trees."

In a partially cleared space, they saw two representatives of the Ba-a-a family.

"You must not take these as specimens of Australian sheep. Not much wool on them! They will look real baggy though, after a while. My wool-shed paddock is pretty big, and has about fifteen hundred acres ·in it, but I guess you have seen enough for one day, and to-morrow you shall see more."

"Do you find much game about here?" asked the captain.

NOT MUCH WOOL ON THEM.

"Oh yes; a kangaroo hunt is quite exciting. I was out last week."

"You have some nice dogs."

"Oh yes, I am a great dog-man, and have a big family of various kinds and sizes, when you put them together. It is one of my hobbies."

After the return to the house, came a season of very hospitable feasting. Then all spent the evening on the veranda, that was made very comfortable with its lounging-chairs and sofas. The boys went to bed early. Before jumping into his nest, Ralph looked out of the window. It was a still, starry night. All around the house, standing a little way off, as if to respectfully recognize the presence of their master's mansion, was a shadowy line of trees.

"And on the other side of the world is old Concord. I wonder what they are doing there!"

After this soliloquy, Ralph turned to the bed. He was wondering whether he had better inaugurate a pillow-fight with Rick, when he heard a snoring.

"Nonsense, he's gone to sleep! I'll put it off till morning," and having made this resolve, Ralph sprang into bed to pass his first night in bush-land. He was awake early the next morning, only to find that though he had a bed, he lacked a bed-fellow. Rick had gone.

"That's mean!" exclaimed the disappointed knight of the pillow. He hastily dressed and went out-doors. The sun was already looking over the wall of gum-trees beyond the house, making an early inspection of the grounds. Ralph went to the kitchen, which was quite near the house.

"Have you seen my brother, a boy not so big as me?" he asked the cook.

"I guess I have. I gave him a lunch, and I guess he has gone down to the wool-shed; for he went that way."

"The wool-shed!"

"Oh, he is all right," and the cook turned a piece of steak she was broiling.

"Uncle Nat won't like that," thought Ralph.

Uncle Nat though was fast asleep, and when he did awake, answering the ringing of a big house-bell, he told Ralph at the table that they were all going after breakfast to the wool-shed, and he added, " I miss Rick, but I guess the young man from Concord is there."

Breakfast over, Mr. Bright and his guests were speedily on their way to the wool-shed.

" That's my wool-shed," said Mr. Bright finally, pointing out a long, low wooden building. " Stop one moment. About here I found, one day last week, my child, away now visiting. The little thing does like sheep, especially a plump little sheep, and the liking seems to be mutual. When missed the other day, my child was found down here, fast asleep, a lot of sheep close by and on guard, I suppose, while their keeper had a nap. Oh, I was going to tell you about my paddocks! Outside this that hems in my wool-shed, are paddocks for the sheep when at large, one having fifteen thousand acres and two others have ten thousand each. Then I have a smaller paddock where my cattle are."

" Do you have a fence round all these? " inquired Uncle Nat.

" Oh yes, miles of it; fifty, we will say. Sometimes it is a 'chock and log' fence; that is, logs resting on blocks, and sometimes it is of bushes laid lengthwise, and then fastened down by forked sticks. Now if a run, as we call it — a range of ground for feeding sheep — should not be fenced, then I must have shepherds to look after my flocks, and the sheep must be penned up at night. If a run is fenced, I have what we call boundary-riders, each rider having at his disposal a couple of horses, and he rides about, looking after both sheep and fences, and sometimes he must trot lively. There is a boundary rider."

They saw on the outer edge of the wool-paddock a man on horseback.

" There is a character I have met in the United States, that they would

"THE KEEPER OF THE SHEEP FAST ASLEEP"

335

call an outrider — a kind of cousin to your boundary rider. It is a similar style of being," said Uncle Nat.

"Come into my wool-shed, please. My men finish shearing about Christmas-time, and they are still at work," said Mr. Bright.

"The sheep have been washed in the wash-pool. It is not anywhere near, but after this first step in the process of wool-stripping, they are driven here. They next are taken into these pens in the shed — see, some have been driven in already, and there go the shearers for their booty!"

The shearers would make a dive for the sheep, bring them out to "the board" or floor, and in a very short time clip "Ba-ba's" coat of wool from the back.

"Tar!" shouted a shearer.

"What does that mean?" asked Ralph.

A COUSIN TO YOUR BOUNDARY-RIDER.

"The shears clipped too close and cut the skin of the sheep, and we put the tar upon the wound," explained Mr. Bright.

A boy with a tar-pot now came hurrying up and gave the wounded spot a plaster at once.

"After the removal of the wool," said Mr. Bright, "a man called a 'sorter,' takes it and gives it a place according to its merits. When the wool has been sorted it is packed into bales, which are then pressed, and finally loaded on wagons that will need a dozen bullocks, maybe, to haul them to some place of transportation."

"Tar!" shouted a shearer.

There was no response.

" Tar! *tar!*" he called again.

"Tar! *tar!* TAR! TAR!" he screamed angrily to the tar-pot boy. He now rushed up, and another wound was poulticed.

" That boy was tar-dy," suggested Uncle Nat. They stood watching the shearers, when Uncle Nat exclaimed: " But where's Rick? I expected to see my nephew down here, Mr. Bright."

" The men say a boy has been here, cap'n, and I guess it was Rick. and he probably went home again."

" Then we shall find him at your house?"

But Ralph had a suspicion that his venturesome brother was not there, and when Uncle Nat returned to the house, Ralph lingered to make a hunt for Rick. Where could Rick be?

Rick had left the house, crazy to get off into the bush and see if he could not find a kangaroo. He wandered through the home-paddock, and then down to the wool-shed where a shearer and a tar-pot boy saw him, and he then turned as if going back to the house, only to digress from the path and strike off among the trees.

" I mean, I mean," soliloquized Rick, " to have a real live kangaroo, all to myself, and I'll make him hop. Yes, I will; see if I don't! And if I should come across a baby-kangaroo, I might nab him and take him home alive, and show him to mother and Nurse Fennel! Wouldn't all the boys in Concord flock to my barn? I tell ye! And they would come from Lexington, too!"

It was still early, and Rick sauntered off among the trees. He soon struck a cart-path through the bush, and presently heard the sound of wheels. A man came along riding in a buggy, and not far behind was a bullock-dray, piled with bales of wool, and making its way to market. Then all was still, save as Rick heard in the bush a cockatoo screaming, or the mournful tones of the magpie.

"Lonely," he said to himself. "Guess I will turn back to the wool-shed."

But where were the kangaroos, and especially that much-coveted baby-kangaroo ? Nothing turned up, and our hunter walked slowly back to the wool-shed.

"What a nice tree," he said. "I wonder if I couldn't climb that ! I don't believe Ralph could !"

Anxious to gain an imaginary victory over Ralph, who was not there to win a real one for himself, Rick wriggled his way up among the branches of the tree, and silently perched on a limb to meditate on the possibilities of securing a baby kangaroo. In a little while he noticed a movement over the ground. Something was there. Was it an animal stealing toward his tree ? It certainly was. His heart began to flutter, when suddenly up among the top branches, such a noise was made ! It was a combination of a bray and a laugh and a hoot ! Ralph's heart went quicker than ever. In his fright, he made a misstep, and fell a few feet to the ground. It did not hurt him ; but what was the matter with the creature he had seen strangely moving toward his tree ! Lifting itself and standing on its hind legs, it gave a tremendous jump and bounded away.

"Oh dear ! massy !" screamed Rick, repeating an exclamation sometimes heard in Concord. Away went the kangaroo in one direction, and away went the kangaroo-hunter in another ! Both were thoroughly scared, and neither dared to look round.

"I wish I had his legs !" thought Rick. Finally, hearing no sound of pursuit, he stopped.

"Whew ! Wasn't that a lucky escape, and won't I have a lot to tell the boys at home ! Been as nigh a kangaroo as that !"

Rick felt that he had covered himself with glory, and could now return contented. Coming in sight of the wool-shed, he went on till he saw the path from the house, and this he followed awhile.   In his weariness, he turned aside to a lonely corner of the paddock to rest. Throwing himself down upon the ground, he thought how nice it would be if he had beneath his head one of mother's "soft pillows," and as he thought, his head sank lower and lower, his eyes shut — but let us turn back to hunt up Ralph.   He first went into a paddock, where a drove of cattle had been turned loose.

" They are not coming this way, I hope," he said to himself.

They were, however.   Whether they considered Ralph as a keeper that might be on the way to them, announcing the arrival of a first-class , meal, no one could say.   Ralph did not relish this welcome from such a lot of big-breasted, horned creatures.   Just then, a dog ran out from the bush near by, and began to bark.   It was a ridiculous contrast — that pert canine, with his small, shrill bark, and those burly oxen!   It diverted the oxen, though, and gave Ralph time enough to gain a fence near by and go over it.   The dog followed, and then wagging his tail, looked up in Ralph's face, as if saying, " Come, now!   If you should guess could you possibly tell who I am?   Did you ever see a dog of my size with this kind of tail that goes so so?" and here the dog gave an extra flourish of his tail.

" Paws ! " shouted Ralph ; " old Paws that I knew in Sydney ! Why, old fellow, where did you come from?   Ah, now I know.   Mr. Bright says he bought a dog in Sydney lately, and you must be the one.   Come, will you help me hunt up my brother Rick?"

Paws wagged his tail, which meant " Let me think of it."   Then he wagged it furiously, which meant, " Yes, yes, yes, I'll go with you."

Crossing now into the wool-shed paddock, what did Ralph see on the ground?   It was the tired kangaroo-hunter !   Ralph knelt down, and laying a hand on Rick's shoulder, began gently to shake him. " Wake up, Rick ! "   The bare-headed hunter raised his head, and opening his eyes, grinned at his finder. The next instant Paws bounded forward, wagging his tail and greeting the now prostrate Nimrod of the bush.

Rick proudly narrated his adventures.

"WAKE UP, RICK!"

"But I tell you, Ralph, I heard a fearful noise up in the tree. It would have scared *you*."

"Did it sort of bray, and hoot, and laugh at you?"

"Oh, yes ; that's it."

"Pooh! I wouldn't let that scare me! That's what they call the laughing jackass, or great kingfisher!"

Rick subsided.

CHAPTER XXXIX

A QUEER COUNTRY.

BEES! BEES!

"M OSQUITOES!" ex- claimed Rick. "Mosquitoes in December? That seems like turning things upside down."

"Yes," said Mr. Bright, "it is a sign that summer indeed has come in Australia. The whole insect-tribe is on the wing, and you will find that mosquitoes are very partial to new-comers! Plenty of flies, too; oceans of them; and bees too, what a quantity!"

"Uncle Nat told us," said Ralph, "that Australia is a queer country, for various reasons, and among others, for the creatures that were here, and I guess we must set down mosquitoes as one. Anything else, please?"

Mr. Bright was obliging as a dictionary, and told all he knew.

"As your uncle said, our country is queer, on account of its creatures. We can't boast of leopards or tigers or lions. We can't scare up a wolf that I ever heard of. About the most destructive thing on four legs that we have is the dingo or wild dog. He worries the sheep fearfully. The dingo has a big, bushy tail and pointed ears, and makes you think somewhat of the fox. They go in packs and yell at night hideously. They steal out of their holes in the hills or where the scrub

342

is thick, and rush upon the flocks. A flock of several thousand sheep chased by dingoes will become much alarmed, and away they go, trampling down the weak ones, and scattering over miles of ground, troubling the shepherds to gather them again. The squatters or settlers

ALL ABOARD FOR A SUNRISE LAND.

try to poison out the dingo, and the animal has received many severe doses. Then we have kangaroos."

"The kangaroos! Oh, don't I want to see a kangaroo jump again!" cried Ralph.

Rick was silent.

"Plenty of chances, boys, if you want to see a kangaroo. They count up many species in Australia and Van Diemen's Land. You know their fore legs are very short and their hind legs are very long, which makes them tremendous on the jump, and they can make such leaps that it must be a very smart horse to keep up with them."

"Well, how do they defend themselves?" asked Ralph.

"Every animal has some means of defense, just as a mean little mosquito has its sting. The long legs so good for jumping, help

ON THE JUMP.

the kangaroo to get away from an enemy, and if the enemy comes near, he may get a stroke from those same hind legs, that carry three long claws, and can rip up a foe very cleverly. The dogs that are accustomed to hunt kangaroos, are very careful just how they tackle them. Then they may seize an enemy with their fore paws, jump to a water-hole and drown it. Why, those fellows I have known to clear a rod at a jump! They are sometimes pretty long, you

THE BLACK SWAN.

know. I saw a full-grown male that from nose to tip of tail measured nine feet. A kangaroo may be no mean enemy."

Rick here drew a long breath, and said to himself: "Guess I don't want a baby-kangaroo." In a moment he spoke up: "But what about their basket?"

"Oh," laughed Mr. Bright, "you mean the mother's pouch, in which she carries her young? You may well call it a basket. We have a good many animals here in Australia that like to carry their young that way. I have seen the young ones looking out of a kangaroo-mother's pouch contented as birds in a nest, or babies in their cradles. I said there were various kinds of kangaroos. Rat-kangaroos, for instance, are about as big as a rabbit, and there are tree-kangaroos, whose fore legs are about equal to the hind ones, and they can go up trees pretty quick. I suppose you boys have seen an animal flying from tree to tree, the flying phalanger, or generally called the flying squirrel; it is known as the flying opossum also. It belongs to the marsupial or pouch family, of which we have at

LYRE-BIRD.

least one hundred and ten varieties in Australia. The flying squirrels have a membrane of skin extending along the hind and fore legs, and it

A FAMILIAR CREATURE.

keeps them up in the air so that they can take long leaps. There is our 'laughing jackass,' a bird that makes a queer noise, and is really the great kingfisher. They call it the settler's clock, for it cries or brays at an early hour, and at sunset."

Ralph looked at Rick and smiled, but the hero of the kangaroo-hunt found it convenient to be watching something overhead.

"Then there is the emu, a tall bird with long legs, and reminding you of the ostrich; and there is the black swan. The black swan was thought by the ancients to be an impossibility, but Australia furnishes it. Then we have that funny creature, which so puzzled naturalists, the duck-billed animal, for it is an animal: the platypus, it is sometimes called. When it was first exhibited, it was thought to be a manufactured prodigy, but they might have concluded that the animal was none too queer for us. It is

THE BOWER-BIRD.

often called the water-mole. It has a bill, as I said, but then, it is not as with a bird, a part of the skeleton, for it is only attached to the skin and muscles. It is a kind of cheat that it hangs out. It can swim and dive like a duck, or it can climb a tree. It burrows under ground and sometimes for twenty or thirty feet, the door being under water, and the chamber for its nest is high up above the water. A queer fellow and a cunning one, too! Then we have a big lizard down this way, the iguana. I have shot 'em five feet long,

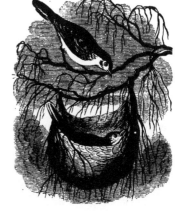

HAMMOCK-BIRD.

and in Queensland there are alligators. We have bats, a creature familiar to you, parrots, eagles, magpies and so on. You ought to see our lyre-bird — or lyre-pheasant — and it is so-called, because its tail-feathers spread in the form of a lyre. We have plenty of snakes, and can furnish any quantity of insects. Our ants, we think, are remarkable, some being an inch long. For an ant, the bull-ant is tremendous.

A BIG BIRD STALKING TOWARD HIM.

"We have not been satisfied, though, with what Australia can furnish, and that alone, for we have been introducing foreign favorites — pigs, deer, sheep, horses, cattle, thrushes, larks, and let me not forget the sparrows. There, I almost forgot — "

Here Mr. Bright arose, and going to a book-shelf took down a volume.

"I came pretty near forgetting some birds I wanted to show you pictures of. We have about seven hundred kinds of birds in this country, and I ought to tell you of one or two more. There is the bower-bird. The spotted variety build on the ground. Twigs are used, outside, but within long grasses are so placed that their tops almost touch. Then they ornament the ' bower' with bits of glass, shells and other objects, sometimes using pebbles they have carried a great way. There is the hammock-bird, its nest swinging from the twigs like a hammock."

Rick went to bed, his head full of birds, birds, birds. What wonder that in a dream he saw a big bird stalking toward him! He was glad to have a tall grass-blade, behind which he could retreat. And even then the winged creature threw a big eye round the corner and made his hair stand on end, as she looked him out of countenance.

THROUGH THE WILDS OF AUSTRALIA.

352

TRADING WITH THE ABORIGINES.

CHAPTER XL.

THE INTERIOR OF AUSTRALIA.

"HARK! What is he saying?" asked Rick. "That man talking to Uncle Nat?"

"Yes."

"He's telling about selling goods to the natives."

"You see, cap'n," said the man, "we traders can sell considerable to the aborigines, and I rather like the fun. We drive into their country and peddle clothing, groceries or nicknacks out of our teams."

"Can't I go, uncle?" asked Rick eagerly.

"Go where?"

" Go to see the bore — bore —"

" Aborigines," said the elder brother.

"No, no; we must be going home. It is past Christmas now," replied Uncle Nat.

Yes, Christmas was over.

" A year ago," said Uncle Nat to the boys, "I was in old England, and we had snow enough for a good time snow-balling. I saw love-making and snow-balling going on at the same time in a park. But Christmas here! Has any one an iceberg they can rent to me for a cool retreat?"

All the world over, whether the Christmas-star shines on fields of green grass or fields of white snow; on waters that run warm and sparkling to the sea, or rivers held fast in frosty chains, it is still Christmas, — the blessed birthday of the Saviour. The *Antelope Guild* passed a happy festival in Melbourne, and soon after the *Antelope* began a race over the waves to Hong Kong. Life on board ship was all the more agreeable for the late interruption, and it was pleas-ant for Ralph and Rick to see once more each day the doctor, Misses Wayland and Percy, Jack Bobstay and Siah. The *Antelope Guild*, too, resumed its meetings, and at the first one the doctor was the lecturer.

"We only have a slight idea of Australia, by seeing it as it is on the sea-board. What was farther back, embraced within its vast coast-lines, was a mystery, and to some extent is a mystery still, but daring explorers have been tempted into searching the interior, and something has been ascertained about it Some explorers were success-ful, and others failed. Pitiful cases of ill-success were those of Leichhardt, who has not been heard from, and of Wills and Burke, dying of starvation in the wilderness. Stuart succeeded in traversing the country, and in his footsteps stretches the long telegraph wire, binding also together the north and south coast of Australia, and

CHRISTMAS IN OLD ENGLAND.

links the country to the outside world. To the east of the telegraph wire is the larger part of that which is settled country. There are fertile lands sweeping far away toward the east, but toward the west is 'a great lone land,' as described by an explorer — 'a wilderness interspersed with salt marshes and lakes, barren hills and spinifex deserts.' Across the lower part of this wild, unknown land, Eyre, afterwards famous as a governor of Jamaica, resolved to make a journey.

"In one place he came to an immense, swamp-like tract, its mud covered with a thin coating of salt. They tried to get through it, going six miles into this bog, but they came near sinking, and gave up the effort. It was a terrible journey for man and horse. Once, they had only three quarts of water to last six days, and part of this evaporated, and part of it was spilled. A dew falling, Eyre gathered up a little of the moisture on a sponge, and his black boys took rags also and wiped up the dew. Eyre met with terrible obstacles in the humanity that travelled with him, two proving to be traitors, robbers and murderers, and he was finally left with a black boy, his only companion in that terrible land. He pushed ahead, though. His privations were great, but he persevered, reaching the west coast. This indomitable spirit spent a year and more in this effort.

"In 1874, John Forrest started to lead a party across the wild, rough interior. Leaving the western coast, for days and weeks they traversed a fine, grassy country, but by and by they struck a dry, miserable land, whose great production seemed to be spinifex, a coarse bush with long, pointed leaves. The surface was frequently flat — one level mass stretching far away. Sand and rocks abounded. Water was the great pressing want of the party. Sometimes they would find it in what they termed 'rock-holes,' and then again these natural wells would be empty. They dared not go back, for there was the same scarcity of drink. 'Spinifex everywhere,' said Forrest; 'a most fearful country.' Tired, sore, their mouths parched, they found enough water in some clay-holes to last about a night. Their rations needed replenishing. What could they do in this emergency? At last the cheering news came that water had been found five miles away, while red kangaroo, one or two opossums, and other game, helped out their larder. So they toiled on. A thousand miles from the settlements in West Australia,

KANGAROO AND BABY.

the prospect was no more cheering; still they pushed forward. They had had occasional meetings with natives, one party being delighted to find that two of Forrest's men were black, and that their bodies also were marked, and that one had his nose bored! The explorers came again to grassy country, and struck the river Marryatt. Their stock

CHRISTMAS IN AUSTRALIA. 359

of provisions was reduced to flour; but it was a sign that they were getting near the end of their wearisome journey.

" One Sunday they looked up and saw a long, fine wire, stretching away on poles. It was the telegraph! They swung their hats in the air, and gave cheer after cheer! They followed the wire, and reached a telegraph station, where they dined on roast beef and plum-pudding! Forrest thinks he traversed an immense tract that never will be settled. There are grassy patches, but too isolated for use. It is a wonder to him that he got through at all, as a drought was drying up the country. We comment by saying, We are not so sure about the correctness of Forrest's opinion concerning inner Australia. The gold veins of Australia may run up into the ' lone land,' and, if that be so, miners will hunt them out, and towns will be gathered there. We can but hope."

CHAPTER XLI.

"ON THE MORROW," said Uncle Nat one evening, "we shall see China."

It was a beautiful night. On and on, across a sea of silver, sped the *Antelope*. A glorious half-moon hung in the sky. Did it mean fair weather?

Another day came. Would it bring them to land?

"China! China, boys!" Uncle Nat sang out.

"Where?"

"Away, away over there, Ralph. Come here and stand behind this mizzen mast. Keep your eye a little to the right; don't you see a hump of blue away beyond the sea?"

"As if a whale had stuck his back up there?"

"That's the spot."

"And that is China?"

"The Flowery Land, and nothing else, unless I am very much mistaken."

"China! China!" shouted Ralph from the quarter-deck, and

362

Rick, who was in the cabin below, came tumbling up and out, crying :.

"China! China! Snapping crackers!"

The boys stood watching the little hump of blue, as if expecting every moment it might turn into a Roman candle or a rocket, and out would burst pigtails and wooden shoes and teachests. But no such explosion took place. The little hump was a fixture on the horizon, gradually growing larger and darker, larger and darker, and by and by there was an unmistakable ridge of land sloping up the western sky.

ON AND ON, ACROSS A SEA OF SILVER.

The breeze stiffened, and the *Antelope* sped swiftly over the waters.

"We are bound for Hong Kong, Rick," said Jack Bobstay a·

little later, "and we shall drop anchor in harbor 'fore the sun sets."

"Have you been there?"

"Oh, yes," said Jack with an air of indifference, as if going to Hong Kong fifty or sixty times in a year even, was a matter of very little consequence. "To go to Hong Kong is gettin' to be rather common nowadays," affirmed this world-renowned traveller.

Who would have supposed such an amount of cosmopolitan experience was under the roof of that battered old tarpaulin? Uncle Nat now approached.

"Hong Kong is an island, and not so very big, either. It is nine miles long and from two to six wide. You will see that parts are pretty high — eighteen hundred feet, at least, above the sea, and the city of Victoria is hilly, as you will notice. The harbor has quite a pretty entrance, and we will have a sail among some islands."

The *Antelope* was hailed by a Chinese pilot-boat or sampan; the home of the pilot and all his family.

"Me sailee up to Victoriee," said the pilot to Uncle Nat, and he winked his dark eyes in a rapid, funny, good-humored way. Coming to its moorings, the chain-cable of the *Antelope* went clanking into the water, and there, after a long race from Australia, the vessel rested as if in the bottom of a deep cup, the hills all about it. The boys looked off and saw Victoria, a city that had a European look, sloping up a hill-side, street rising above street, like a succession of terraces. There were steamers at their wharves, while around the *Antelope* lay many sailing vessels at anchor.

"What a funny ship that is, Uncle Nat?" said Ralph.

"That is a Chinese junk. You see what a high poop or stern she has, and how they have built up her forecastle."

"Are those eyes?" said Rick, catching a look at her bow.

"Yes; they carry two big eyes."

" So that they can see ? "

" I suppose so."

The junk's two big eyes amused Rick exceedingly.

As the sun went down behind the hills of Hong Kong, it seemed as

A CHINESE JUNK.

if on their summits a huge bonfire had been started, whose embers were
then scattered in glorious confusion by the Chinese boys, the light playing through and over the broken clouds. Then the fire seemed to
descend from the western sky, and flashed again from the windows of
the city, tier of light succeeding tier of light. When the boys went to
sleep that night, they could hardly realize that they were in the China.

they had read so much about ; the land where the men wore long hair, and braided it like women ; the land where women hobbled about on

feet so funnily shaped ; the land of fireworks and kites ; the land of the mighty wall, and the land of Aladdin and his wonderful lamp. Rick in his dreams that night thought he was a stout Chinese youth blessed with a pigtail and stealing up to a shrine where burned tne mystic lamp.

"And now, boys," said Uncle Nat, "I am going to Victoria, and you can

A CHINESE RICK AND THE LAMP.

go with me. We will leave the doctor here with the ladies."

Dr. Walton seemed willing to stay behind and keep the ladies company, especially Miss Lissa. So Ralph judged.

"All ready, boys?" shouted Uncle Nat. "We will take a sampan."

There were plenty of sampan-proprietors about the ship that were willing to take the party ashore, and the voyage was soon over.

When the boys stepped on land, Uncle Nat told them that they were in Victoria — the great business centre of Hong Kong.

"I hope, boys," said Uncle Nat, "I shall find in his office a man whom I want to see."

But the man was not in his office.

"He is at his house," said the clerk.

"Then we must go to his house," declared Uncle Nat; "and, boys, don't you want to ride in a sedan-chair?"

The boys were ready for any novel sort of a vehicle — a sedan-chair, an elephant's back, a camel's hump, a balloon, or the tail of a comet.

"Here, Rick; here, Ralph; a chair for each of you! Pop in, boys; pop quick!"

"See those girls!" said Ralph.

"Can't stop to look at females now; pop in," cried Uncle Nat, and in they popped.

They found that a sedan-chair was a kind of box sporting a top, and in the box was a caned seat. This odd style of vehicle was suspended from two long poles that rested on the shoulders of two bare-legged Chinamen wearing immense hats.

"When, boys, you want them to go faster, say 'chop-chop!' When you want them to go slower, say 'man-man!' They will understand you."

"All right, uncle," replied Rick.

In a few minutes Rick said mildly, "Chop-chop."

The bearers quickened their pace. Rick was as delighted as young Phæton when he drove the horses of the sun.

"Chop-chop!"

They went faster.

"Chop-chop!"

Once again they stepped more briskly.

"Chop-chop!"

Faster.

"Chop-chop!"

Faster yet.

"Halloo, there, Rick; say man-man!"

It was Uncle Nat bawling, but Rick no more heard him than the hum of a fly a mile distant.

"Chop-chop!" went Rick in unconscious response to the distant fly-hum.

Faster.

"Chop-chop!"

They were now turning a street corner, when, suddenly — was it an elephant, a man-of-war, or a clap of thunder, that Rick's bearers had struck? They had abruptly come to a halt, and some others in the opposite direction had concluded as suddenly to stop, and there was a good deal of Chinese jargon in the air. In the midst of all this babel appeared a stout, red-faced old gentleman, bobbing out of a sedan-chair and proclaiming in very vigorous and very intelligible English: "Somebody is a fool!"

Added to this was the childish voice of Rick piping in high tones, as he leaned forward: "I beg pardon, sir! My men didn't know you were in the way."

"Your *men*," replied the old gentleman; "if a *man* had been inside that concern of yours, this collision wouldn't have happened."

There now appeared on the scene Uncle Nat, who had been bawling himself hoarse as he shouted "man-man!" to Rick's enterprising team.

"Rick, what are you up to? Oh, Mr. Wadham, is this you?" he continued, addressing the old gentleman whose chair had been run into. "We were going up to your house."

"Well, sir, a few minutes ago I didn't know as I should ever see home again. But who — who — " here the old gentleman rubbed his eyes. "Bless me, who is this? Why, Capt. Stevens, how are you? Come right up to my house;" and the old gentleman grabbing Uncle Nat's hand, began to work it up and down as if a pump-handle and he were trying to fetch water.

OUT-DOOR SCENES IN CHINA.

"Thank you, Mr. Wadham. We shall be right glad to go. And I hope you will excuse my nephew Rick. Rick, why didn't you stop when I called ' man-man ' to you ? "

" I didn't hear you, uncle, and they seemed willing to go."

" Willing ! ", observed the old gentleman. " Those boobies are glad enough to get a foreigner into a scrape."

"I beg your pardon, sir," said Rick courteously.⁻ ⁻ " I did not see you, sir."

" Oh, let it go. Those boobies don't know anything."

Having relieved himself of his indignation in his opinion about the Chinese, half-ashamed, also, of himself for making so much of the matter, Mr. Wadham whispered to Uncle Nat: " Fact is, cap'n, I tried that very same thing myself the first time I had a chance, years ago."

He now returned to his chair, and the procession moved away toward his house.

Rick having enjoyed the sense of motion, now prepared to exercise the sense of seeing. He noticed that the street was bordered by quite good looking buildings covered with a grayish-brown cement. On the door-step of one house, he noticed a little girl, to whom an old

citizen of the Flowery Land was giving — was it an orange or a lime ?

The sedan-chairs were quite near one another, and Mr. Wadham called out: "We will go into the Public Garden, if you would like, for I want you to see the view."

And what a view down upon the harbor, dotted with shipping and encircled by hills!

"Now we will go to my house. Chop-chop, every man of you!" And away went the bearers.

Mr. Wadham's house was built of stone, and around it swept broad verandas. In the garden that enclosed the house, were odd, big-leaved plants, clumps of box, also, that had been cut into the forms of animals and plants, while on the borders of the grounds were rows of bamboos. The house was decorated with many Chinese curiosities, while comfortable, also, and attractive with English furniture.

HONG KONG WOMAN.

"There's a Hong Kong woman," softly whispered Mr. Wadham to Uncle Nat, as they passed by the opened door of a room. "You know we have a good many Chinese on the island. This is a friend of my wife's."

The lady was seated near a little fancy table, holding a fan in her hand.

Mr. and Mrs. Wadham were very hospitable, and insisted that Uncle Nat and the boys should stop to dinner. At the table, the waiters were all Chinese, and dressed in cool, white garments, and they served up roast beef, cooked in English style, curried chicken, and various Chinese dishes. By the time the ice-cream was brought, the boys were ready to say that they would like to live in Hong Kong. The Hong Kong woman was shy of visitors, and they did not see her again ; but her little girl was ready to entertain them. She had acquired some knowledge of the English, and stood by a chair and interested the company with her bright sayings, though the medium of their expression was, pigeon-English. But that,

A YOUNG CELESTIAL.

however, is the Chinaman's deficient way of speaking our language.

CHAPTER XLII.

CANTON.

IMAGE OF CONFUCIUS.

"A ND what do you think of this, boys?" asked Uncle Nat.

"Funny, Uncle Nat," replied Rick, with eyes wide open and laughing.

They had taken a steamboat, and were gliding up the Pearl river, that leads to Canton. At last, leaving the steamer, "for the sake of variety," as Uncle Nat said, they chartered a sampan for the rest of the journey. This boat was a home for a family of five; a man and his wife and three children. Here, in their snug quarters, roofed over with matting and bamboo, they lodged and lived. The man, having a job on shore, was absent, but the mother and two stout boys managed the craft.

"These folks live here all the time, Uncle Nat?" asked Ralph.

"Certainly, Ralph; and they tell me there are eighty thousand of the Canton people living in boats. In these floating homes they are born, live and die."

Canton is a big city, uncle ? "

" Yes, it is estimated to have a million of people."

As they neared the city, the crowd of sampans, junks and steamers increased, and the boys were glad to escape with Uncle Nat from the din and confusion on the river, and to charter sedan-chairs.

" Chop-chop ! " shouted Uncle Nat, and off started the bearers. The streets were long and narrow, and those they visited. did not have a width exceeding eight feet, and some were only four feet wide. The houses were rather small, not containing more than two stories, as a rule. On the first floor oftentimes was a shop, and the goods for sale would be on exhibition and open to inspection. Once in a while they met an officer riding a pony, but the sedan-chair was the favorite mode of passenger-travel, and goods were suspended from bamboo-poles that rested on the shoulders of patient bearers. Sometimes a shade would stretch between opposite houses in a narrow street, sheltering those below.

" Boys, I want to show you a temple or two, if I can make my bearers understand just what we are after. We will go first to the temple of the five hundred genii," said Uncle Nat.

They were carried to it, and found it to be an immense structure containing images of the five hundred genii reported to be devoted servants of Buddha, while they lived.

" There's Buddha's image, boys," called out Uncle Nat, " and it is gilded. It makes you think of Japan."

The boys were not very much charmed. Then they hunted up a temple of Confucius.

" You remember, boys, you learned in Japan about Confucius. Here is an image of him, which does not look very genial and agreeable," said Uncle Nat.

" If I had time, we would go to see the temple of the Five Genii.

It is said that their names were Fire, Earth, Water, Wood and Metal; and that these five worthies once came to the city riding on rams, and a blessing very naturally came with them."

"And you can't see the rams, Uncle Nat, can you?" asked Rick.

IMAGE OF BUDDHA.

"Oh, yes, though they had changed to stone the last time I saw them, and I guess they have not run away since. But there is a place I think we must go to."

"What is this other place?" asked Ralph.

"Examination Hall ; and we will see it."

"Chop-chop!" Off they all went. By and by Uncle Nat sang out: "man man," pounding on the side of his chair. The procession halted. Stepping out of the sedan-chairs, and passing through a structure into a court, they saw lengthy rows of buildings, with low roofs, and each building was cut up into little rooms.

"Those little cubby-holes," said Uncle Nat, "make you think of cells in a honey-comb, and you are quite likely to find a bee in each cell at certain seasons. Candidates for office come here by the thousand — men who have passed a previous examination and shown merit in them — and into these little rooms they are locked, each man by himself. He is expected to remain there in seclusion for a while. He is furnished with subjects on which he is expected to write essays and their merits will decide whether the candidate is worthy of advancement. Of the thousands examined not many will take the prize, which is an honorary degree. This gives one the privilege of going to Pekin, and there trying for another degree which, if he receives it, entitles him to a high standing as a literary man, and also gives him a chance to hold some position of trust under government."

"What about those who don't take those degrees?" asked Ralph.

"They give it up, I guess, some of them ; but if they wish, they can try it again in three years, and then keep on trying, if unsuccessful. When an unsuccessful man perseveres in his examinations till he is seventy, perseverance is rewarded, at least, for he receives a degree of honor and some government office."

"They don't do it up as quick as people who want office in America?" said Ralph.

"No; at home the way has been for a man to carry round a piece of paper asking for office till the paper was well-covered with big names, and well-soiled with ink, and if he could have a 'friend at court,' to shove his petition and make a noise for him, he was likely to get an office that would pay him for his trouble. But we are doing a little better nowadays; we are beginning to make merit a condition that must be met. There is any amount of room still for improvement. Now we will look into some of the shops. Chop-chop!"

When the chairs halted again, Uncle Nat suggested that they alight, and make a visiting tour on foot.

"Here is a strange street, boys — the Street of the Dead. Here are to be found things that the living are generally interested in, and the Chinese think that the spirits of their departed friends will still be interested in such articles. So they buy a pipe, or a fan, or

A CHEAP UMBRELLA.

some other memento, and pack these into the coffins or tombs of the dead."

"That is very funny," thought Rick.

"A pipe is the last thing I want to be packed away with me," said Uncle Nat.

They rambled on, till Ralph cried out: "Oh, see that man making umbrellas!"

The umbrella-maker was busy at work, putting together a light bamboo-frame, and then neatly stretching over it a big cover of varnished paper.

"Sometimes they use oiled paper," said Uncle Nat, "to cover the frame. They have all grades of materials for umbrellas, poor and rich, homely and elegant. It makes me think of the time when I saw you, Rick, at Concord. You were big enough to run about the garden and see things for yourself. You came into the house laughing, and wanted us to go out and see 'toadee under umbel.' We went out, and sure enough, there was a toad under his umbrella.

"Among our English ancestors," continued Uncle Nat, "the umbrella was little known down as far as the opening of the seventeenth century. In that century it was used as

LORD OF THE TWENTY-FOUR UMBRELLAS.

a sun-shade. When Queen Anne was on the throne, ladies used the umbrella as a protection against the rain, but only ladies, though. The first man who spread an umbrella in the streets of London, was Jonas Hanway, the philanthropist. He was a sickly man, and an um_

rella was a friend in need. For some time, though, people poked **fun at**
the male user of an umbrella. Now you know they are very common
with the English-speaking people. If all the styles of umbrellas
in Concord alone, say, should take it into their wooden or ivory heads
to get up a procession and walk off, what a sight it would be!

"It is in the East, that the umbrella is used so much, and
there it may signify a good deal. In Siam, it is a sign of rank,
and it may indicate also degrees of rank. A nobleman can carry
an umbrella with a single top, but the king may have a series of
such roofs above his head. When we get to Burmah, the king has
a name derived from the umbrella: Lord of the Twenty-four Umbrellas."

"That would be a two-dozen decker, wouldn't it, Uncle Nat?"
asked Ralph, while Rick thought if the king would stand from under,
his umbrella would be a nice thing to fire snow-balls at, and a sure
pop every time!

CHINESE GIRLS.

CHAPTER XLIII.

JOE PIG-TAIL.

RICK was lost in Hong Kong. One day when ashore with Uncle Nat, the latter said : "Hold on here a moment," and bobbed into an English merchant's office.

"Aye, aye, Uncle Nat," said Rick obediently.

But Rick strayed off, "just a little," as he said, watching a boy with a kite, then a sedan-chair, and then something else, till at last, entangled in a crowd, he lost all idea of the way back to Uncle Nat.

"Oh dear!" he groaned; "I guess I'll take this street," and taking it, he left behind him the stores, and reached the neighborhood of the private residences. He was moving along aimlessly and disconsolately, fancying that somehow he might find Mr. Wadham's residence, perhaps, when he neared a house surrounded with an ample garden.

"I will ask that Chinaman gardener in there if he knows where Mr. Wadham lives, and if he doesn't know perhaps that girl near him can tell; but girls don't know much," thought Rick; "she wears a pretty' hat, though."

Rick shouted, "Can you tell me where —"

The Chinaman turned and faced Rick.

"Why, why Joe Pigtail, that you?" exclaimed Rick, bounding furiously into the garden. The wearer of the pretty hat turned also toward Rick, and at the sight of her sweet face Rick's heart seemed to bound more violently than his legs even.

It was Amy Clarendon! The old acquaintances advanced toward Rick.

"Me gladdee see you," said Joe, bowing.

"And *I* am *very* glad to see you," was the encouraging welcome from the young fairy.

"Isn't this nice? Do you live here?" inquired Rick.

"Yes, this is my father's, and Chung Kang is our gardener," said Amy.

Here Joe Pigtail bowed.

"All the folks are away," said Amy, "and you must stop to dinner, Rick."

What a dinner that was! Rick was thinking he had reached fairy-land, and, finishing a glass of ice-cream, was about to attack another, when he heard a voice in the entry — a voice generally musical enough, but now it sounded like a dragon's:

"He is here, then? I have been hunting for him, and some one saw him come here. Well, please say that his uncle is at the door, and is in a great hurry to get to the ship."

"No help for it," thought Rick. "I must go."

Uncle Nat was glad to see Amy and Chung Kang again, and urged them to visit the ship. The visit was made, and then came Rick's second sorrowful parting from the Clarendons' gardener.

Rick was thinking about the future. "Uncle Nat says the *Antelope*

is going to India and through the Suez canal to Egypt, and then home; and what then? I know what — if I only had Aladdin's lamp they tell about! I would turn our barn — if mother would give it to me — into a palace, and Amy should live in it with me. And then, what if Uncle Nat and the doctor should fancy those nice ladies that are our passengers, and marry them! Perhaps we might all live in Concord and Aunt Fennel adopt Jack Bobstay as her son, and Bumble-bee cook for us, and Siah be our coachman! Wouldn't that be just splendid?"

Two days after, the *Antelope* erected her fair white antlers, and was bounding away for the next port. Rick went to sleep that night, and dreamed again of the palace he could create if only the wonderful lamp were his. Alas! do our dreams often come true?

THE END.

Lightning Source UK Ltd.
Milton Keynes UK
UKHW011502110119
335397UK00010B/400/P